The Death of Vivek Oji

The Death
of
Vivek Oji

AKWAEKE EMEZI

faber

First published in the USA in 2020
by Riverhead Books,
an imprint of Penguin Random House LLC

First published in the UK in 2020
by Faber & Faber Ltd
Bloomsbury House
74–77 Great Russell Street
London WC1B 3DA

Printed and bound by CPI Group (UK) Ltd, Croydon CR0 4YY

*This is a work of fiction. Names, characters, places and incidents are either
the product of the author's imagination or are used fictitiously, and any
resemblance to actual persons, living or dead, businesses, companies, events,
or locales is entirely coincidental.*

A CIP record for this book
is available from the British Library

ISBN 978–0–571–35098–8

FSC
www.fsc.org
MIX
Paper from
responsible sources
FSC® C020471

1   3   5   7   9   10   8   6   4   2

To Franca, my first and best storytelling friend.

Don't ever forget Kurt's last name.

I love you lots.

Live free.

One

They burned down the market on the day Vivek Oji died.

Two

If this story was a stack of photographs—the old kind, rounded at the corners and kept in albums under the glass and lace doilies of center tables in parlors across the country—it would start with Vivek's father, Chika. The first print would be of him riding a bus to the village to visit his mother; it would show him dangling an arm out of the window, feeling the air push against his face and the breeze entering his smile.

Chika was twenty and as tall as his mother, six feet of red skin and suntouched-clay hair, teeth like polished bones. The women on the bus looked openly at him, his white shirt billowing out from the back of his neck in a cloud, and they smiled and whispered among themselves because he was beautiful. He had looks that should have lived forever, features he passed down to Vivek—the teeth, the almond eyes, the smooth skin—features that died with Vivek.

The next photograph in the stack would be of Chika's mother, Ahunna, sitting on her veranda when her son arrived, a bowl of udara beside her. Ahunna's wrapper was tied around her waist, leaving her breasts bare, and her skin was redder than Chika's, deeper and older, like a pot that had been bled over in its firing. She had fine wrinkles around her eyes, hair plaited into tight cornrows, and her left foot was bandaged and propped up on a stool.

"Mama! Gịnị mere?!" Chika cried when he saw her, running up the veranda stairs. "Are you all right? Why didn't you send someone?"

"There was no need to disturb you," Ahunna replied, splitting open an udara and sucking out its flesh. The large compound of her village house stretched around them—old family land, a whole legacy in earth that she'd held on to ever since Chika's father died several years ago. "I stepped on a stick when I was on the farm," she explained, as her son sat down beside her. "Mary took me to the hospital. Everything is fine now." She spat udara seeds from her mouth like small black bullets.

Mary was his brother Ekene's wife, a full and soft girl with cheeks like small clouds. They had married a few months ago, and Chika had watched Mary float down the aisle, white lace gathered around her body and a veil obscuring her pretty mouth. Ekene had been waiting for her at the altar, his spine stern and proud, his skin gleaming like wet loam against the tarred black of his suit. Chika had never seen his brother look so tender, the way his long fingers trembled, the love and pride simmering in his eyes. Mary had to tilt her head up to look at Ekene as they recited their vows—the men in their family were always tall—and Chika had watched her throat curve, her face glowing as his brother lifted up the tulle and kissed her. After the wedding, Ekene decided to move out of the village and into town, into the bustle and noise of Owerri, so Mary was staying with Ahunna while Ekene went to set up their new life. Chika stole a glance at Mary from the veranda as she watered the hibiscus garden, her hair tied back in a frayed knot, wearing a loose cotton dress in a faded floral print. She looked like home, like something he could fall into, whirling through her hips and thighs and breasts.

His mother frowned at him. "Mind yourself," she warned, as if she could read his mind. "That's your brother's wife."

Chika's face burned. "I don't know what you're talking about, Mama."

Ahunna didn't blink. "Go and find your own wife, just don't start any wahala in this house with this girl. Your brother is coming to collect her soon."

Chika reached out and took her hand. "I'm not starting anything, Mama." She scoffed but didn't pull her hand away. They sat like that, another picture, as the evening pulled across the veranda and sky, and something boiled slow and hot in Chika, thrumming at the back of his throat. This was before Vivek, before the fire, before Chika would discover exactly how difficult it was to dig his own grave with the bones of his son.

When Ahunna's wound healed, it left a scar on the instep of her foot—a dark brown patch shaped like a limp starfish. Her son Ekene came and took his wife to their new house in

Owerri, a white bungalow with flame-of-the-forest growing by the gate and guava trees lined up by the fence, and Chika visited them there. These would be the happy pictures: Mary smiling in her kitchen; Mary plaiting her hair with extensions and singing with her full throat in her church choir; Mary and Chika gisting in the kitchen while she cooked. Ekene had no patience for talkative women and he wasn't the jealous type, so he didn't mind that his junior brother and his wife got along so well.

As for Chika, the thing boiling inside him took on a new heat whenever he was around Mary. It sang and bubbled and scalded him where no one could see. He joked to his family that he just liked being in a house with a woman in it, rather than his empty bachelor flat, and Mary believed him—until one afternoon when he stepped behind her as she was cooking and put his mouth on the back of her neck. She whirled and started beating him with the long wooden spoon she was using to make garri.

"Are you *mad?*" she shouted, flecks of hot garri spitting off her spoon and burning the forearms he'd raised to block her blows. "What do you think you're doing?"

"Sorry! Sorry!" He dropped to his knees, bowing his head under his arms. "Biko, Mary, stop! I won't do it again, I swear!"

She paused, breathing hard, her face confused and hurt.

"What's your problem, ehn? Why must you try and spoil everything? Ekene and I are happy, you hear? We're happy."

"I know. I know." Chika stood up slowly, one reversed knee at a time, keeping his hands up and looking into her eyes. "I know. I don't want to spoil anything. Please, forgive me."

Mary shook her head. "You can't continue coming here if this is what you're coming for." Chika wanted to reach out to her, but her knuckles were tight around the spoon.

"I know," he said, keeping his voice soft.

"I'm not joking," she said. "Don't come back with this non-sense."

Chika looked at the tears hanging wet inside her eyes and he put his hands down.

"I hear you. I swear, from now on, you're just my sister." He felt her eyes on him as he reached for his car keys. "I'm going. I'll see you next week. Please, let's just forget today, okay?"

Mary said nothing. She just watched as he left, her fingers relaxing against the curved wood of the handle only when the door closed behind him.

For the next several months, Chika kept his distance from Owerri. He got a job as an accountant at a glass factory in Ngwa, the market town he had moved to when he left the vil-lage. The company doctor there was Dr. Khatri, a pale Indian man with shocks of gray hair at his temples. Sometimes, Dr. Khatri would bring in his niece, Kavita, to help with adminis-trative work. The first time Chika met her, he'd gone in to see the doctor about a cough and Kavita was at the front desk with files heaped around her, frowning as she flipped through them. She was a small woman with dark brown skin and a thick braid of black hair hanging past her waist. That morning, she was wearing an orange cotton dress; she looked like a burning sunset, and Chika knew immediately that his story would end with her, that he would drown in her large liquid eyes and it would be the perfect way to go. There was nothing boiling in him, just a loud and clear exhale, a weight of peace wrapping around his heart. Kavita looked up and smiled at him, and somehow Chika found the liver to ask her to lunch. It surprised them both when she said yes, as did the affection that unfurled between them in the weeks that followed.

When it became apparent how serious their courtship was getting, the doctor invited Chika to their home, where Kavita served them tea and small bowls of murukku. Her wrists were delicate, and her dark hair rained off her shoulders. Dr. Khatri told Chika how, after her parents died, Kavita had passed into his care, eventually coming with him all the way from India to Nigeria. "We had some . . . family problems back in Delhi," he said. "Because of her father's caste. It was better to make a fresh start." Chika nodded. That was the same reason he chose not to live in the same town as any of his family. Fresh starts were good; that separateness was where you could feel yourself, where you could learn who you were apart from everyone else.

Picture: the young couple in the back garden after dinner, walking along a line of bare rosebushes, Kavita running her fingers gently over the branches.

"I can't wait for these to bloom," she said. "I used to hate the smell of roses back when we lived in Delhi, but my uncle loves them, and now—it's strange—all they do is remind me of home."

Picture: Chika's hand covering hers, serrated leaves crushed under their palms, a quiet kiss where their breaths tangle.

―――――

Afterward, Chika went to the village and told his mother about Kavita. "I want you to meet her," he said, avoiding her eyes. Ahunna watched him, his bent shoulders, the way he kept taking his hands out of his pockets and putting them back in. Children never really change, she thought, no matter how much they grow up.

"Bring the girl," Ahunna said. "Nsogbu adịghị." She went back to peeling yam, sitting on a low stool in front of the basin holding the tubers, throwing the rind out into the backyard for her goats. Chika stood above her, a dazed smile spreading across his face.

"Yes, Ma," he eventually said. "Daalụ."

It was only then he finally felt ready to visit Owerri, to share the news with Mary and Ekene, now that he could go to their house with a clean conscience. He and Mary never spoke of what had happened, that moment of misplaced desire in a sweltering kitchen.

Three months later, Chika proposed to Kavita in the rose garden at her uncle's house. By then, pink and red blooms filled out the branches and the air was thick with scent. Kavita smiled, blinking back tears as she threw her arms around his clay neck and kissed him yes. A few days later, the families started arguing about the dowry. Chika tried to explain to Dr. Khatri that it was the husband's family who paid the bride-price, but the old doctor was enraged by the very idea. "We came all the way from India with Kavita's dowry! It is her inheritance. I cannot let her go without it as if she's worth nothing to us!"

"And I cannot accept a brideprice from my wife's father!"

Hearing that word—*father*—Dr. Khatri teared up, and their argument hiccupped. "She is truly a daughter to me," he said, his voice thick.

Ahunna rolled her eyes and stepped in. "You men like shouting too much. Just let the dowries cancel each other, and no one pays anything." Dr. Khatri drew in breath to protest, but she held up a hand. "You can keep Kavita's dowry for her children. I don't want to hear pim about this again."

So that was that. Kavita's dowry was a small collection of heavy gold jewelry that her mother had brought into her own marriage, passed down through the women before her.

Picture: Chika with Kavita in their bedroom, newlywed, the heavy necklaces and bangles pouring over his hands. "I don't even know what to say. It's like the treasure you read about in books."

Kavita took them from him and returned them to their box. "For our children," she reminded him, not knowing there would only be one. "Let's just forget it's even here."

Most of the jewelry stayed in that box for the next two decades, nestled against the deep red velvet, gemstones and gold links gleaming in the dark. There were times when Chika and Kavita sold one small piece or another, when things were difficult, but they held on to most of it, planning to use it to send their son, Vivek, to America. But when the jewelry finally came out of the box, it was Vivek's hands that lifted it.

Picture: the boy, shirtless, placing necklaces against his

chest, draping them over his silver chain, clipping his ears with gold earrings, his hair tumbling over his shoulders. He looks like a bride, half naked, partially undressed.

There is another boy in this picture now. His name is Osita. He is as tall as Vivek, but broader at the shoulders, his skin like deep loam. He is Ekene's son, born of Mary, and his eyes are narrow, his mouth full beyond belief. In this picture, Osita's face is carved and dark with alarm. He stands with his arms folded, his jaw set against something he cannot predict.

Vivek smiles at his cousin with gold droplets falling into his eyebrows. "Bhai," he says, with a voice like a bell. "How do I look?"

Osita wished, much later, that he'd told Vivek the truth then, that he was so beautiful he made the air around him dull, made Osita hard with desire. "Take it off," he snapped instead, his throat rough. "Put it back before they catch us."

Vivek ignored him and spun around. There was so much light trapped in his face, it hurt Osita's eyes.

"I would do anything," he said, after Vivek's burial, "give anything to see him like that just one more time, alive and covered with wealth."

The market they burned down used to be just after the second roundabout if you drove down Chief Michael Road, past the abandoned office buildings and the intersection with the vulcanizer, that short man with a scar breaking his right cheek. His name was Ebenezer and he had been working at that junction for as long as anyone could remember. Kavita used to bring their family car to him when the tires needed repair. It was a silver-gray Peugeot 504, which Chika had bought after years of working at the glass factory, replacing the old rundown car he'd been using. As a child, Vivek would place a small palm against the hot metal of the car, balancing from foot to foot as he watched Ebenezer work. The scar was thick against Ebenezer's skin, a shiny clotted red pushing out from the brown of his face. When he smiled at Vivek, the scar fought the folding of skin and his mouth rose properly on only one side.

"Small oga," he used to tease, as his hands moved metal wrenches and tubes and force-fed air. Vivek would giggle and hide his face in Kavita's skirt. He was young then, alive. Kavita could drop her palm and it would fall to the back curve of his boy skull, the soft hair and the warm skin underneath, the formed bone shaping him. Years later, when she found the length of his body stretched out on their front veranda, under four yards of akwete material in a red-and-black pattern she said she'd never forget, the back of his skull was broken and seeping into her welcome mat. Kavita lifted his neck anyway, to press her cheek against his and scream. His hair fell over her arms, wet and long and thick, and she wailed.

"*Beta!*" she screamed, her voice carving the air. "Wake up, beta!"

One of Vivek's feet was twisted sideways next to a fallen flowerpot, soil spilled around his ankle. Everything smelled of smoke. His shoeless feet revealed the scar on his left instep: a soft starfish, colored in deep brown.

On the day Vivek was born, Chika had held the baby in his arms and stared at that scar. He'd seen it before—Kavita always commented on its shape whenever she rubbed Ahunna's feet. Kavita had been without a mother for so long, her love for Ahunna was tactile and rich with childlike affection, a hundred thousand touches. They would sit together, read together, walk in the farm together, and Ahunna would give thanks that she'd given birth to two sons and been gifted two daughters. When Ekene and Mary had their child Osita, Ahunna had wept over his little face, singing to him in soft Igbo. She couldn't wait for Chika and Kavita's baby to arrive.

Now it was a year later, and Chika felt something building in him slowly as he held his newborn son—like folds of pouring cement hardening into a sick fear—but he ignored it. These things were just stories; they couldn't be real. It wasn't until the next day that a messenger boy from the village came to Ngwa to tell Chika that Ahunna had died the day before, her heart seizing at the threshold of her house, her body slumping into her compound, the earth receiving her slack face.

He should have known, Chika told himself as Kavita screamed in grief, Vivek clutched to her chest. He did know. How else could that scar have entered the world on flesh if it had not left in the first place? A thing cannot be in two places at once. But still, he denied this for many years, for as long as he could. Superstition, he said. It was a coincidence, the marks on their feet—and besides, Vivek was a boy and not a girl, so how can? Still. His mother was dead and their family was bereft, and in the middle of all this was a new baby.

This is how Vivek was born, after death and into grief. It marked him, you see, it cut him down like a tree. They brought him into a home filled with incapacitating sorrow; his whole life was a mourning. Kavita never had another child. "He is enough," she would say. "This was enough."

Picture: a house thrown into wailing the day he left it, restored to the way it was when he entered.

Picture: his body wrapped.

Picture: his father shattered, his mother gone mad. A dead foot with a deflated starfish spilled over its curve, the beginning and end of everything.

Three

Osita

Vivek chipped my tooth when I was eleven years old. Now, when I look in a mirror and open my mouth, I think of him and I feel the sadness crawling through me again. But when he was alive, when it first happened, seeing it just used to pump anger through me. I felt the same after he died, that hot anger, like pepper going down the wrong way.

When we were small, he and I were always getting into fights. It was mostly nothing, scuffles here and there. But one day, we were pushing each other in his backyard, our feet sliding in the sand under the plumeria tree, both of us angry over something. Vivek pushed me and I fell down against a concrete soakaway outside, splitting my lip, and that was when my tooth chipped. I cried, then was ashamed of crying, and refused to speak to him for a few days. He was about to leave for boarding school up North—some military academy that De Chika had insisted on, even though Aunty Kavita begged him for months not to send Vivek. But my uncle wanted him to toughen up, to stop being so soft and sensitive. I wanted him to stay, but I was too angry to tell him. He left and I stayed behind, nursing an injured pride that prompted me to fight anyone who brought up the missing corner of my tooth. I fought a lot in school that term.

By the end of the year, I missed him terribly and I started to look forward to when he would return home to Ngwa during the rainy season on holiday. It was during one of those long breaks that Vivek's mother convinced mine to enroll us both in SAT prep classes.

"It'll get the children ready for American universities," Aunty Kavita said. "Then they can get scholarships and an F1 visa. Think of it as straightforward."

She and De Chika expected Vivek to go overseas for university, with a certainty they passed down to him—a knowledge that his time here at home was temporary and that a door was waiting as soon as he was done with his WAEC exams. Later I realized that it was the spilling gold of the dowry that funded this belief, but back then I thought they were just being optimistic, and it surprised me, because even my own mother who believed in thick prayers had never mentioned me going overseas. The gold was a secret door, a savings account that could buy America for Vivek.

I didn't want to take the test prep classes, but Aunty Kavita begged me. "Vivek won't do it unless you do," she said. "He really looks up to you. You're like a senior brother to him. I need him to take the classes seriously." She patted my cheek and nodded as if I'd already agreed, giving me a smile before she walked away. I couldn't say no to her and she knew it. So every Friday and Saturday during the holidays, Vivek and I took a bus down Chief Michael Road to the test center. I got used to spending the weekends at Vivek's house, to the Saturday breakfasts when De Chika would detach the cartoon section of his newspaper for Vivek and me, when Aunty Kavita made yam and eggs as if she'd been doing it her whole life.

She had learned to cook Nigerian food from her friends—a group of women, foreign like her, who were married to Nigerian men and were aunties to each other's children. They belonged to an organization called the Nigerwives, which helped them assimilate into these new lives so far away from the countries they'd come from. They weren't wealthy expats, at least not the ones we knew. They didn't come to work for the oil companies; they simply came for their husbands, for their families. Some knew Nigeria because they'd lived here for decades, through the war even; others spoke Igbo fluently; between them, they taught Kavita how to cook oha soup and jollof rice and ugba. They held parties for Easter and birthdays, and when we were little, I used to follow Vivek to attend them. We would line up for the photograph behind the birthday cake; we dressed up as ninjas for the costume party and spent weekends in the pool with the other Nigerwives' kids at the local sports club.

One year, when we were all around thirteen or fourteen, there was a potluck at Aunty Rhatha's house. She was from Thailand and had two daughters, Somto and Olunne, roundfaced girls who laughed like identical wind chimes and swam like quick fish. Her husband worked abroad, but Aunty Rhatha seemed to get along just fine without him. She made pink and yellow cupcakes, fluffed with air and sugar, decorated with carefully piped designs and sugar decorations, birds and butterflies in startling colors. Though he had a bit of a sweet tooth, Vivek hated the cupcakes, but he took his share anyway so he could give it to me. We walked around the house as wings melted in my mouth, our bare feet against the cool marble tile. Aunty Eloise was pacing in the back parlor, on the phone with someone, probably one of her sons, who had already left for university in the UK. Eloise was short and plump, with thick sandy hair and a perpetual smile. She and her husband, a doctor from Abiriba, both worked at the teaching hospital, and Aunty Eloise liked to host dinners and parties at her place, just to get some sound back into the walls now that her children were gone.

"Why doesn't she just go and join her kids?" Vivek wondered aloud.

I shrugged, peeling a cupcake wrapper off. "Maybe she likes living here? Or maybe she just likes her husband."

"Please. The man is so dry." Vivek looked around, at the other Nigerwives clustered in the dining room, arranging pans of curry and chicken and rice along the table. "Besides, most of them are only here because of their children. If not, they would have left from since." He snapped his fingers for emphasis.

"Your own mother, nko?"

"Mba now, her own is different. She was already living here

before she got married." We heard the front door open and Aunty Rhatha's high voice, shimmering as she greeted the new arrival. Vivek cocked his head, trying to hear the guest's voice, then smiled wickedly at me. "I think that's Aunty Ruby," he said, wagging his eyebrows. "You know what that means—your girlfriend is here." I was grateful he couldn't see me blush through my skin, but his eyes were laughing at me anyway. Aunty Ruby was a tall woman from Texas who owned a day-care center; her husband owned a carpet shop, and her daughter, Elizabeth, was one of the most beautiful girls I had ever seen in my short life. She was a runner, lean and longboned, with a swaying neck. I once tried to beat her at a footrace but it was useless, she moved like the ground was falling away beneath her feet, the future rushing toward her. So I stood back and watched her race all the other boys in the area who thought they could take her on. Elizabeth always won, her chest high and forward, sand flying behind her. Most of the boys were afraid to even talk to her; they didn't know what to do with a girl who was faster than them, but I always tried to chat with her a little. I think it surprised her, but she didn't seem to like me the way I liked her. She was always nice to me, though, if a little quiet.

"Leave me alone, jo," I said to Vivek. "Is it because Juju is not here?"

Vivek colored immediately, and I laughed in his face as Somto and Olunne came around the corner with a bowl full of sweets.

"Do you want?" Somto asked, her voice bored as she held out

the bowl. She hated when her mother hosted things, because they always had to help set up and serve and clean afterward. Vivek shook his head, but I rifled through the bowl, picking out the Cadbury chocolate eclairs that were my favorite.

Olunne stood next to her sister, twirling the white stick of a lollipop around in her mouth. "What were you talking about?" she asked.

"His wife," I said, grinning. "Juju."

Somto kissed her teeth. "Tchw. Please. I don't have energy to waste on that one."

"Ah-ahn," Vivek replied, "what's your own?"

"She never comes to these things," Somto complained. "The rest of us have to attend, but that one just lets her mother come alone. Who does she think she is, abeg." Somto was right: Jukwase, who we all called Juju, didn't like to come to the Nigerwives' events. Her mother was Aunty Maja, a nurse from the Philippines who was married to a much older businessman. I'd watched Vivek pine after Juju for years, but the girl was too somehow, a little strange.

"Maybe she thinks she's too janded to be here," Olunne said, shrugging. Juju had been born overseas, even attended school there for a few years before her parents moved back to Nigeria. She'd been very young at the time, but her voice still kept an accent that was different from ours. It was too easy to gossip about her, especially when she avoided the rest of us.

"Don't mind her, she's there forming fine girl because of her hair," Somto said, her lip curling. I bit my tongue; this hair thing was a sore point for Somto, who'd had to cut hers the year before when she started secondary school. Juju's mother had enrolled her in a private school that didn't require mixed girls to cut their hair, so Juju got to keep hers long, curling down her back. Vivek frowned, but he knew not to push Somto or defend Juju too hard. It wasn't until we were on the way home that he lowered his voice to complain to me.

"The girls don't give Juju a chance because they're so jealous. It's not fair."

I nodded, knowing how it had cut at him to hear them talking about her. "It's not," I agreed, mostly for his sake. He just liked that girl too much. She lived down the road from De Chika's bungalow, at the end of a quiet street near Anyangwe Hospital. We used to ride our bicycles up the street all the time, slowing down when we passed Juju's house. Aunty Maja loved flowers, so their fence was covered with piles of pink and white bougainvillea.

"Go and knock on the door," I told Vivek. "See if she's home."

"And say what?" he replied, pedaling in slow loops in the middle of the road.

I shrugged, confounded by the intricacies of wooing a girl in her father's house. We pedaled home, leaving our bikes next to the swing set in the backyard. There was a cluster of bitterleaf bushes in front of the boys' quarters, fighting with an ixora hedge for space. Aunty Kavita and De Chika used to have a househelp who lived there, but she returned to the village after a year or two—a death in the family, I think—and they never replaced her. Vivek and I took over the housework; we would sweep her old room in the boys' quarters as if someone still lived there, dragging the broom under the metal frame of the bed. We stayed there when we wanted to be away from the grown-ups, our bodies sprawled over dusty-pink bedsheets, eating boiled groundnuts and throwing the shells at each other. Aunty Kavita left us alone there, only shouting from the back door of the main house if she needed anything. De Chika never even set foot inside. All of this made it a little easier for me to hide Vivek's thing from them when it started.

I don't know how long it had been happening before I noticed. Maybe someone else noticed first and just didn't say anything, or maybe no one did. The first time I saw it with my own two eyes was the year after he chipped my tooth, on a Sunday after I had gone to Mass with them. It was afternoon, and Vivek and I hadn't even changed out of our church clothes. We'd eaten lunch, cleared the table, then escaped to the boys' quarters with a small stack of Archie comics that Aunty Eloise had brought back from her nephews on her last trip to London. I had one splayed out on the cement floor, my head and one arm dangling off the edge of the bed, my feet propped against the flaking wall. Vivek was sitting cross-legged on the mattress beside me, his comic in his lap, spine curving forward as he bent his head over the pages. The day was hot and quiet, the only sound the rustling of thin paper and an occasional cluck from the chickens outside.

Vivek's voice broke into the silence, low and rusty. "The wall is falling down."

I lifted my head. "What?"

"The wall is falling down," he repeated. "I knew we should have fixed the roof after it rained last time. And we just brought the yams inside."

I closed my comic and sat up. His head was still bent but his hand was unmoving, resting on a half-turned page. His fingernails were oval, cut short down to the beds. "What are you talking about?" I asked. "Are you all right?"

He raised his head and looked right through me. "You don't hear the rain?" he said. "It's so loud."

There was nothing but sun pouring through the glass louvers and old cotton curtains. I stared at Vivek and reached my hand out to his shoulder. "There's no rain," I started to say, but when I touched the cotton of his shirt and the bone of his joint underneath, his eyes rolled up into white and his body flopped sideways, falling against the mattress. When his cheek hit the foam, he jerked as if he was waking and scrabbled his arms and legs, pushing himself back up and gasping loudly. "What? What happened?"

"Shh! You're shouting," I said. I didn't touch him because I was afraid of setting him off again.

His eyes were wide and jittery. He looked around the room, his gaze brushing past me as his breath settled. "Oh," he said, and dropped his shoulders. Then, almost to himself, "This thing again."

I frowned. "Again? Which thing?"

Vivek rubbed the back of his neck, looking uncomfortable. "It's nothing. Just small-small blackouts. Forget it."

I kept looking at him but he wouldn't look back at me. "You were talking about rain," I said. "And yams."

"Ehn?" he replied, cramming an is-that-so into one sound. "I don't remember. Biko, fashi the whole thing." He picked up his comic and lay on his side, turning away from me. I didn't say anything, because that's how he was: when he wanted to stop talking about something, he stopped talking about it, shutting down like metal protectors had fallen around him. But I watched him, after that—I watched him to see if it would happen again.

There were moments when he would become very, very still, just stop moving while the world continued around him. I saw it happen when we were leaving class one evening: Vivek stopped walking and our classmates jostled and pushed him as they filed past. I was a few people behind him but he still hadn't moved by the time I caught up. The others were glaring at him, sucking their teeth as they shoved past. He was walking as if he was drunk, staggering and stumbling, his lips moving slowly and soundlessly. I grabbed his elbow and propelled him forward, pulling him against me so he wouldn't fall. As the stream of people continued out of the compound—JAMB exams were coming up, and the test center was full of students—I got Vivek through the gate and pushed him out of the way, up against a fence by the roadside gutters. Finally, he shuddered and came back.

"Are you all right?" I asked, letting go of his elbow.

He looked at me and the protectors fell over his face. "I'm fine. Let's go." I followed as he strode toward the bus stop, wary but silent.

Somehow it became like that whenever he was back from

school, even when we went to the village house over the holidays, me watching him close and intervening when I could and Vivek never really telling me what was going on. If I stepped in like I had at the prep center, he just thanked me and we'd continue as if nothing had happened. I got used to it.

None of our parents noticed, maybe because he was always so controlled around them, never as relaxed as he'd been in the boys' quarters. To them, it just looked like he had quiet spells. Aunty Kavita would assume he was tired and tell him to go and sleep. My mother told her to check if he was anemic, and Aunty Kavita fed him large portions of ugu for a while, just to be on the safe side. He and I still read our comics and ate boiled groundnuts in the boys' quarters of his house when I was in town; we still rode our bikes down the street; we still knocked down guavas and mangoes with a hollow bamboo stick, then lay on the bonnet of De Chika's car to eat them.

We were young, we were boys, the years rolled by in the heat. Later, much later, I wondered if I should have told his parents what was going on, if that would have helped him, or saved him a little.

Two years before I finished secondary school, I finally gathered enough courage to approach Elizabeth. She was taking the SAT classes with us and I toasted her the same way we all toasted the girls we liked—I bought her FanYogo after class and escorted her to the gate when her driver came to pick her up.

Vivek watched me and laughed. "You're finally chyking this girl?" he said. "Thank God. At least you didn't wait until graduation."

After a week of sending her letters and carefully writing down the lyrics to the hottest love songs for her, Elizabeth finally agreed to be my girlfriend. She saved the letters, all written on sheets of foolscap paper torn out of my exercise books, and wrote me notes telling me how romantic I was. I visited her house in Ngwa a few times—I already knew I could never bring her to Owerri.

One weekend, she suggested traveling down with me when I was going home.

"I have an aunty who lives there," she said. "And my parents know your aunty, so they'll allow me to go with you. You know how the Nigerwives are." She was starting to get excited about the idea. "We can take the bus together!"

I refused. I didn't want to chance anyone seeing us together at the bus stop in Owerri and reporting me to my mother. She had already warned me about having girlfriends during a rant about the sins of the flesh, when she told me that if she ever caught me masturbating, she would throw me out of the house. I couldn't believe she was the one talking to me about that instead of my father, but my mother didn't care. By then, she was a hardened pillar of religious fervor and prayerful discipline. When De Chika told me stories about the cheerful young woman my father had married, the one he used to sit and gist with in the kitchen, I couldn't recognize her as my mother. The mother I knew was a straight-mouthed person who held nightly prayer sessions, always kept her hair wrapped in a scarf, and quoted her pastor in every second breath.

Meanwhile, my father was staying longer each day at the office and I was spending more weekends at Vivek's house, even when we didn't have SAT classes. My mother noticed this immediately, of course. How could she miss it when we were all she had? She complained to my father about his absence, and when he continued to stay late at work, she decided he had a mistress. It was a fear fed to her by the women in her church. Why else, they reasoned, would he stay away from his family? No, he had to be keeping some girl in a guesthouse somewhere. On the nights I was home, I sometimes heard the shouting from their room as she threw accusations at him in tight, balled-up words.

"You think you can just go and take another woman, ehn?! And me, I will fold my hands and allow it? Tufiakwa! You will tell me who she is, Ekene—today today! You will not sleep until you tell the truth and shame the devil!"

"Mary, lower your voice," my father said, his voice tired and level. "The boy is asleep."

"Let him hear!" she said, her voice punctuated with claps. "I said, *let him hear*! Is this how you want to shame me in front of everybody? Oya now, let us start with our son!"

I covered my head with my pillow to block the sounds.

"Your mother wants you to spend more time here," my father told me the next morning over breakfast. "This is your home. Not your uncle's house."

I kept my mouth shut and ate my cornflakes, even though I

wanted to tell him that he was just as guilty as me. He was never there. He was the one leaving me alone with my mother, who felt like a hammer instead of a person. So I stayed away from home when I could, making up an impressive roster of excuses: De Chika was sick and they needed me around the house. The road from Ngwa to Owerri was plagued with armed robberies and it wasn't safe to travel. If my mother had simply told De Chika that she wanted me home more, he would've sent me along immediately, but she never brought it up and he didn't notice how often I was around. I think my mother kept quiet because she didn't want it to look as if she and my father couldn't handle me.

Aunty Kavita had told me once that my mother had wanted more children, but that she'd stopped trying after several miscarriages. I couldn't imagine what she'd gone through—how much of my mother's life I missed because I was a child—but I wondered if that was what changed her. She must have prayed so much in those years. Maybe that's where the bright, high-spirited woman De Chika talked about went; maybe she'd been sanded down into dullness by grief and prayers that went unanswered.

Instead, she held on to her faith with a stubborn kind of bitterness, as if it were all she had left—a trapped and resentful love. Who could stay bright and bubbly after losing baby after baby? What do you do when you're not allowed to be angry at God? I could see why she made everything so heavy, but I still ran from her, all the way to the boys' quarters at De Chika's house and to Elizabeth, who made me never want to go back to Owerri.

"I don't like to be in my house either," she told me. Her family didn't have a lot of furniture, and although Elizabeth said it was just the style, I had heard my aunt and uncle talk softly about her father. He was a quiet man, gracious, always with a handkerchief in his suit pocket, but from what I'd overheard, he was also a drunkard. His carpet store was always in danger of closing—he spent their money as if it was water—and Aunty Ruby had to hide what she made at the daycare center from him. Elizabeth never talked about it and I never asked her. She let me come over when he wasn't home, but she preferred to visit me at De Chika's house, in the boys' quarters.

"I like it here," she said, twirling around the room. "It's like our own little world." My heart pounded as I gazed at her arms and legs, so long and brown, sticking out from her clothes, ending in narrow hands and sandaled feet. There had been one or two girls at school that I'd knacked before, but Elizabeth was the first girl I'd brought there, to that small room and the dusty-pink bedsheets. She never stayed more than an hour or two; Vivek came looking for me there after his piano or French lessons, and she would always straighten her clothes and leave before he returned. I spent what time we had in disbelief that this person—the same one I used to watch as she cut through the air running—was here, choosing to be with me. I remembered in exquisite detail how, each time she won a race, her face would light up, her lips parted as she panted for breath, her eyes bright with victory. I wanted to re-create that look. I wedged the door to the boys' quarters shut and pushed up against her, and she giggled under my hands and mouth. "Don't stop," she sighed, as I kissed her neck. Her skirt was starched and green and pleated. I slid my hands up her thighs, but she pushed them away, so I just held her waist instead.

One afternoon we were making out on the bed, our hips grinding through layers of clothing, when Elizabeth pulled her head back and searched my eyes with hers. "Touch me," she whispered, and I froze, wondering if I'd heard her correctly. She let her legs fall open and arched her hips up toward me. "Touch me," she said again, and I obeyed, reaching under her skirt. We fucked right there on the mattress—the sweat of her body against mine, her legs around my waist—and it was like a better life. My hair was short then, but I kept it in little twists like I was trying to start dreadlocks. She slid her hand into my hair and tugged on it, and the pain in my scalp was electric and perfect. I had to strip the sheets afterward to hide where I'd pulled out and spilled all over them.

Two hours later, I lay on the bare yellow foam of the mattress and told Vivek about it, about the noises she made and how she felt inside. He was standing by the window in a green T-shirt, leaning on the wall, eating chocolate Speedy biscuits from a purple packet he held tight in his hand.

"You didn't use a condom?" he asked, making a face.

I shrugged. "Abeg, I wasn't prepared. How I fit know today was the day the babe go gree?"

"That's stupid," he said, his voice flat.

"Small boy," I sneered, a little stung by his comment. My cousin was a virgin and I knew it. He scuffed his foot and looked out of the window. There was a dark bruise around his right eye. I sighed and changed the subject, gesturing at his face. "Oya, who was it this time?"

"That Tobechukwu idiot from next door. Feels he can just open his mouth anyhow and talk rubbish." He flexed his skinned knuckles and ate another tiny biscuit. It had been years since he'd chipped my tooth, but Vivek still fought a lot, just with other people now. He had a temper like gunpowder packed into a pipe, a coiled-up strength that had developed with time, and because he was thin and quiet, no one expected the violence to explode out of his frame the way it did. I had seen a couple of his fights, and they were worse than when he used to fight me. At first, I'd tried to break them up, but I stopped after I arrived late once and saw Vivek beat the living hell out of the other boy. He didn't need my help.

"Where did the two of you fight?" I asked, surprised he hadn't gotten into trouble.

"Down the road."

"You're lucky his mother didn't see you. What did your mumsy say when she saw your face?" I knew Aunty Kavita would have been upset.

"She hasn't seen anything," he snapped. "Fashi that one. Gist me about Elizabeth. How many times?"

I grinned. "Back to back," I boasted. I didn't tell him how it had felt when she gasped my name into my ear, her fingers digging into my back—like in that moment I was a whole entire world.

Vivek rolled his eyes. "It's here you've been bringing her?"

"Yes, but it's just today we did that," I said.

He glanced down at the speckled foam of the mattress. "Is she going to come here again?"

"Maybe. What's your own?"

Vivek ran a hand over his shaved head, the skin like burnt gold. "I want to watch next time," he said, lifting his chin at me.

I sat up on my elbows, my chest bare, still smelling of her and sex. "Wait, wait," I laughed. "Repeat yourself."

He raised an eyebrow and kept quiet. I flopped back down on the mattress.

"You dey craze," I said, looking up at the popcorn ceiling. "Watch for where?" I sucked my teeth.

"I'm serious," Vivek said. "Unless you want me to tell my father what you've started doing back here." I sat up fully and stared at him, but he was holding back a smile and laughed when he saw the alarm on my face. "I'm not going to report you, abeg. I'm just saying you should include me small."

"Why do you want to watch?" I asked. "Is it that you like her or what?"

He scoffed. "I just want to see what all the noise is about. You people that keep talking about this knacking, knacking, every time knacking."

"Ehn? So you want to just collect a chair and sit in a corner folding your hands while you watch us?"

He gave me a sneering look. "Nna mehn, don't be stupid. I can just see through the window."

"And if someone catches you standing outside, nko?"

"Who's going to see me with all those bushes outside the window? I can just stay behind them."

Vivek ate another handful of biscuits casually, as if he was suggesting something normal. I lay back and stared at the discolored walls, trying to imagine Elizabeth being there again, her short hair rubbing against the mattress in rhythm with my thrusts, except this time with a pair of eyes pressed against the torn mosquito net of the window.

"It's not as if you'll see me," Vivek said impatiently, as if he'd read my mind. "Just pretend I'm not there."

I gave in. I actually knew some friends who did things like this. They'd rent a hotel room and some of them would sit and drink on the room's balcony in the dark, watching as the girl got fucked inside, laughing quietly behind the glass of the sliding door, hidden by sheer curtains and the lack of light. We were men together and we liked to show off, so I agreed.

The next week, Elizabeth came back. We sat together on the mattress, my back sweating. Her collar was unbuttoned, showing the stretch of her neck.

"How are you?" I asked, stroking the palm of her hand with a finger.

She smiled at me. "I'm fine. Happy to see you."

"I wasn't sure if you would come back after last time."

Elizabeth laughed. "Why not?"

"Maybe I didn't do a good job."

She gave me a look, and in that second, I saw that she was nowhere as innocent as I'd imagined. I had assumed she was a little inexperienced because she was quiet and played hard to get, so it had felt satisfying to be the one with her on that mattress when we fucked. Like I was accomplishing something. But the way she looked at me made me think maybe I knew less about what was going on than she did.

"If you didn't do a good job, you think I'd be here?" she said, and gave me such a cocky smile that my voice left me for a few minutes.

"So you're just using me for my skills, abi?" I managed to joke, and Elizabeth laughed, throwing her head back.

"Don't worry yourself," she said. "Just enjoy. What's your own?" She leaned in and kissed me and I stopped thinking. I unbuttoned the white cotton of her shirt with my pulse pounding, not looking at the window in case I'd see Vivek's face behind the thin curtains. He'd insisted I replace the sheets on the bed ("Are you mad? You want to fuck her on just foam?"), and that I use a condom ("I don't care if it makes her think you're expecting sex. You are expecting it. And what if she gets pregnant?"). So we washed the pink sheets and dried them out on the clothesline, and now my palm was pressed against them as I tugged at Elizabeth's underwear with my other hand.

She sighed and threw an arm over her face, turning it away from me. I kissed her neck and a breeze from the window made the curtains flutter. I focused on the curve of Elizabeth's ear and her hand came up to grasp the back of my neck, her palm cool and dry. The sounds she was making must have carried through the spaces between the glass louvers. I briefly wondered what Vivek was doing out there. Was he touching himself or what? Isn't that what someone would do? And what if De Chika or Aunty Kavita caught him behind the bushes exposed like that?

Elizabeth wriggled a little under me, dragging my attention back to her open shirt and small breasts cupped in a lace-trimmed cotton singlet. I pulled the neckline down and put my mouth on her nipple, fumbled between our legs, ignoring the condom in my pocket as I pushed and sighed my way into her.

"Nwere nwayọ," she warned.

"Oh!" I braced my hands against the bed and pulled back a bit. "Ndo."

She smiled and kissed me, then wrapped her legs around my waist, her skirt falling up to her hips. We moved gently, and when the pleasure started to get too sharp, I pulled out to catch a breath. Elizabeth laughed and touched my cheek—but then she glanced past my shoulder and suddenly screamed, scrambling to cover herself and pushing me away. I turned around and there was Vivek, standing in the doorway, looking over the room, his eyes hooded and unfocused.

"Jesus Christ!" I leaped off the bed and pulled up my trousers. "What the fuck are you doing?"

He held on to the door frame and didn't reply, his fingers digging into the wood. Elizabeth was crying, pulling her clothes back together, her hands shaking. I shoved Vivek and asked again, louder, but he just rocked backward like rippling water, then flowed forward, staggering a little.

"What is he doing here?" Elizabeth shouted, between sobs of rage. "Get him out!"

I pushed him harder, then again, out of the room, and he just kept taking it, his mouth slightly open, looking like a fucking mumu.

"Chineke, what's wrong with you?" I knew he was having an episode, I knew he was sick, but I didn't care. I was tired of covering up for him, tired of him being sick or strange or whatever was wrong with him. I really liked Elizabeth, you know, and now she was there, angry and crying in a corner of the bed, after he'd been standing in the door watching us for God knows how long. So I pushed him with all the anger I had and Vivek fell off the concrete landing, two steps down onto the ground. He broke his fall as if by reflex, twisting so that his hips and shoulders hit the sand, but his head still rocked from the impact, his eyes were gone, he still wasn't here. Elizabeth screamed and I ran back into the room, terrified that Aunty Kavita would hear her from the main house, terrified that I'd hurt Vivek by pushing him so hard.

"Shh—it's okay," I said, climbing back on the bed and wrapping my arms around her. "It's okay."

"I want to go home," she sobbed.

"No wahala. Come." I took her hand, then led her off the bed and through the door. Vivek was curled up on the sand below, with his hands pressed to his face, hyperventilating. "Don't mind him," I said as we passed. "His head is not correct."

I escorted her out to the main road and she entered a taxi without looking back at me, slamming the door so hard that the frame of the car rattled. I watched it drive away, spluttering black fumes from the exhaust. She was never coming back, I thought in that moment; our relationship was over. I dug my hands into my pockets and walked back to the house, dragging my feet.

When I got back, Vivek was sitting on the landing, his back propped against the door frame.

"I'm sorry," he said, as soon as he saw me, trying to stand up quickly. "I don't know what happened—"

"You know what happened," I said. "I don't even care again. I'm tired. Every time with this your thing."

"Osita, please—"

"I said I'm tired."

He ran a hand over his head, distressed. "What do you want me to do? Should I go and say sorry to her?"

"Don't fucking talk to her," I snarled, and Vivek flinched. I shook my head and raised my palms, backing away from him. "It's enough," I said. "It's enough." I didn't look back as I walked away. I threw my clothes into a bag, then caught a bus back to Owerri, knowing I'd miss the SAT class the next morning. I didn't care.

My mother stared at me when I walked into our house. "You're home," she said, frowning. I hadn't been back in a while. Usually she would shout at me for being away so long, but this time she just looked up at me, her shoulders rounded and tired. She was sitting in the parlor with a tray of beans in her lap, picking out the stones, and she looked like maybe she had been crying.

I put down my bag. "Yes," I said. "I'm home."

Four

Vivek

I'm not what anyone thinks I am. I never was. I didn't have the mouth to put it into words, to say what was wrong, to change the things I felt I needed to change. And every day it was difficult, walking around and knowing that people saw me one way, knowing that they were wrong, so completely wrong, that the real me was invisible to them. It didn't even exist to them.

So: If nobody sees you, are you still there?

Five

After Vivek died, Osita went to Port Harcourt and drank until the days were sabotaged in his memory. He didn't tell anyone where he was going, and when he got there, no one cared about where or what he had come from. He was tall and immaculately dark-skinned, muscled and handsome and generous with drinks, so the oil workers he fell in with were more than happy to spend time with him. There were hotel rooms and some women, and a memory of dirty glasses stacked high and teetering before they crashed into a sink and broke, then the warped sound of people laughing. Osita watched the glass bounce. He felt carpet against his back and tasted a vileness in his mouth, as if someone had vomited into it. A girl straddled his hips and lowered her face to his, but it blurred to nothing.

Then he was floating on an inflation tube in someone's pool, his hands and feet trailing in the water. A bald woman was treading water next to him. "You're crying," she said. It was only then that Osita noticed the tears slipping into his ears. It was evening and the light was leaving. "It's raining," he told her, slurring his words.

She laughed. "It's not raining."

"It's raining inside me," he said, and a wave of darkness took over. When he woke up, he was lying on a pool chair on his stomach, his head turned to the side. There was a small pile of sand on the cement next to him, thrown over his drying vomit. No one else was by the pool. Osita sat up and found a bottle of schnapps that someone had left on the floor. It was still a quarter full.

He drank some more.

He was gone for a few weeks, and they only found him because his aunt came to Port Harcourt looking. One of the Niger-wives there connected Kavita with a taxi driver who knew everyone in town.

"He's tall," she told him. "Very black. Gorimakpa. And one of his front teeth is broken."

After two days, the taxi driver took her to one of the hotels. The receptionist quickly allowed her upstairs because she was Indian and angry and demanding things in a raised voice. When they unlocked a door near the end of the corridor, Kavita walked in to find Osita lying on the bed, snoring loudly, his breath gurgling in his chest. She flinched at the smell of the room and shoved his shoulder. Osita jumped up, grunting in alarm and rubbing his eyes. He hadn't shaved in days; stubble spread from the curve of his skull to his face.

"Aunty Kavita? What are you doing here?"

"Put on your clothes," she said. "I'm taking you home."

He stood up, obeying automatically, even as his head swam. "Give me five minutes," he said, stumbling to the bathroom in his boxers as Kavita watched him. It was impossible for Kavita to see Osita without seeing her son, Vivek—the two of them as boys, sitting together at the dining table, running through her house with their wrestling toys, fighting on the parlor carpet. When she started looking for the small charm Vivek used to wear around his neck and couldn't find it, Osita had been the first person who came to mind.

The charm had been missing since before the burial, but Kavita hadn't wanted to look for it properly then. If she found it too soon, she would've had to bury him with it; even Chika had noticed it was missing. If she found it afterward, she could keep it for herself. She went through Vivek's room looking for it after the burial, but it wasn't there. She called Maja and Rhatha and Ruby and told them to ask the children if any of them had seen it. All of them said no. The only person remaining was Osita, but since Kavita wasn't talking to Mary, she made Chika call Ekene and ask for him.

"We haven't seen him," Ekene said. "We're even a bit worried. He said he was going to Port Harcourt for work but we haven't heard from him since. It's not like him to behave like this. Mary says he was drinking heavily before he left. I don't know what's going to happen to that boy."

Chika had said it was ridiculous to go chasing after Osita. "He's twenty-three, he's not a child anymore," he said. "Leave that man alone." Kavita ignored him and went to Port Harcourt anyway. She had to find that charm.

Now, standing in her nephew's hotel room, she felt a little jealous. If she could have run away and fallen apart like this, doing God-knows-what with God-knows-who, she would have done so in a heartbeat. But she had a husband, and useless as he was, he was something she didn't want to leave, not now.

Kavita heard the water start running from the showerhead, then the louder hiss of her nephew urinating against the inside curve of the toilet bowl. She looked around the room, at the clothes and underwear scattered on the floor, at the empty bottles and condom wrappers, grimacing when she saw a used condom lying next to the bed. Mary would have a fit if she saw this, she thought. Sometimes Kavita missed her sister-in-law, but whenever that pain showed up in her chest, she reminded herself that the Mary of today was not the same Mary she'd known all those years ago. You lost that sister a long time ago; she's gone, just like Ahunna. The only difference is that her body is still walking around.

The sounds of water from the bathroom turned off, and a few minutes later Osita came out dressed in jeans and a T-shirt. Kavita watched him collect his scattered things and stuff them into the suitcase. His embarrassment was palpable as he picked up the condom wrappers and the used condom, tossing them in the wastepaper basket, but his aunt didn't say anything and so, gratefully, neither did he.

"I'm ready," he said, zippering the suitcase and levering it upright. Kavita nodded and Osita looked around the room one more time as they left.

A s they drove out of Port Harcourt, Osita rested his head on the window and fell in and out of sleep, slivers of memory glimmering in his head. The fact of the hotel room was strange—he couldn't remember checking into it in the first place. He'd been relieved to see the condom wrappers, but he only had vague memories of using them. Things had gotten even stranger when his aunt appeared, barely seeming real, but he had followed her as if she was salvation, and now they were going home.

Osita pressed his forehead against the glass of the window as a blurry memory tried to push forward. There had been a man. He rubbed his eyes and tried to place the image. Yes, there had definitely been a man, in that same hotel room. Short and stocky, with hairy muscles. Lebanese. Osita vaguely remembered the man undressing him, then removing his own shirt to expose a firm potbelly. His unfamiliar voice calling Osita beautiful, so black and so beautiful. Osita had been silent, his head swimming, his limbs clumsy. Slivers of memory: The man's sweat matting the hair on their chests as he ground against Osita, a fog of raised voices. Osita's cheek pressed into the mattress, a hand forcing the back of his neck down, the man's hips pushing, seeking. The sound of heavy grunting, a stab of pain, a flare of rage.

In the car, Osita jerked back from the window and looked at his right hand. It was swollen. As he stared at it, dull pain filtering up his arm, he remembered rising up from the bed with a roar, his left hand wrapping around the Lebanese man's throat, then watching the sneering power drain out of his eyes, replaced by a sickly fear. The man had thought Osita was too drunk to resist, but Osita was much taller than him, much bigger, and powered by senseless grief that was ready to evolve into rage. He'd held the man by the throat and punched his face with his free hand in a flurry of short sharp blows that split the man's eyebrow and washed blood down his cheek. The darkness came back, and the next memory was of the man stumbling out of the door holding his clothes against his chest, swearing loudly.

Osita had collapsed onto the bed and Kavita had woken him up. It was, now that he thought about it, a very good thing that she'd come to get him when she did. He had a feeling the Lebanese man would have returned—people don't react well to their power being beaten out of them. He cradled his hand, wondering why he hadn't noticed it while showering. Then, the pain had been diffuse—everything, inside him and out, had hurt—but now it was concentrated and loud. Kavita reached out and gently examined the injured hand, ignoring his wincing. She rummaged in her bag and handed him some Panadol and a bottle of water. "Take," she said. Osita swallowed the tablets obediently. The chasm in his chest was riddled with pain, as his mind compared memories of Vivek's touch with that of the stranger in the hotel room. There had been a party, he recalled now, and all the people had bled away until only the man was left, his greedy hands "helping" Osita to bed. The whole time in Port Harcourt, Osita had fucked only women—it had been like that since Vivek died. It felt safer, as if he wasn't giving any important parts of himself away: not his soul or heart, just his body, which didn't matter anyway. The stranger's assault felt especially violent because of that, and Osita was glad he'd beaten him up.

Fucking foreigner, thinking he could take whatever he wanted. No man had touched him since Vivek died, and the way Osita felt now, perhaps no man ever would again.

He rested his head on Kavita's shoulder. She patted his cheek. "Try and sleep," she said, "there's go-slow." Osita closed his eyes, and they made the rest of the drive back to Ngwa in silence.

The charm Kavita was looking for had been a gift she'd received from Dr. Khatri when Vivek was still a baby. It was made of silver, in the image of Ganesh, and it hung from a thin silver chain. "Give it to your son," he'd said. "Never let him take it off." Kavita could still remember the warmth of her uncle's hands as he pressed it into hers, the octagon of the pendant cutting slightly into her palm. "Promise me, beti."

Even though Kavita had converted to Catholicism, even though the charm was an idol, she had agreed. She kept it for several years, afraid that Vivek would swallow the pendant as a toddler and choke. On the day she finally gave it to him, when he was six, Vivek looked at her with his serious dark eyes and insisted on putting it on himself. His hands moved like a ritual as he lifted the chain over his head and let it drop. From that day on, Ganesh rested just below the hollow of Vivek's collarbone, but it was missing when his body turned up by their front door. After the burial, Chika decided that it must have been stolen, of course it had been stolen—it was silver, real silver, after all, not that plated nonsense. But Kavita didn't want to hear it. It couldn't have been stolen, couldn't have been lost. He must have removed it and put it somewhere.

"He never took it off, woman." Chika hadn't bothered to rise from the bed as he said it, his eyes following her as she rummaged through her dressing table. "Why would it be there? You're being ridiculous."

"Shut up!" she shouted. "You don't know. You don't know what happened. You don't know where he put it! If you don't want to help me, then leave me alone." Chika shook his head and turned over, backing her, leaving her to her madness. Futility had pressed him flat.

Kavita didn't have time to talk to her husband. His friends had been calling the house to see how he was doing; even Eloise called a few times to check on him. All Kavita could think about was finding that necklace. She kept hoping Osita would know where it was.

"You can stay as long as you like," she said when they reached the house. "Help me search his room for the pendant. You know which one I'm talking about? The silver one?"

Osita nodded. "The one with the elephant-head god on it."

"Yes, exactly. If he took it off, he would have put it somewhere safe. I've looked, but I know how you boys are. There

must be somewhere special, somewhere I haven't looked yet."
Her face was lit with a desperate hope.

It made Osita uncomfortable. He knew as well as Chika did
that Vivek never took the pendant off, but he could tell it would
be pointless to say that to Kavita. When they stepped into
Vivek's room, Osita paused at the doorway, his skin skittering.
It was strange to be there, in that new emptiness. He looked at
the wine-colored velvet curtains that blocked out the sun, and
remembered the afternoons they'd spent there—building elaborate wars on the bedspread as children, listening to music,
talking about their crushes. And then, years later, after Vivek
came back from university, those sparse afternoons when they
weren't at Juju's house or in the boys' quarters, when they drew
the velvet curtains closed and lay in the dark, whispering. Now
the air in the room tasted dusty and alone.

Kavita looked back at Osita and he stepped in, scratching
his head. "Erm, maybe here?" he said, walking over to the book-
case. "He used to hide things inside his books."

"Just any of them?" Kavita stood by his shoulder, peering at
the shelves.

"No." Osita pulled down one book: Vivek's copy of *The
Beautyful Ones Are Not Yet Born* by Ayi Kwei Armah. "Usually
just this one," he said, opening it. A dry pressed flower fell out
as he flipped through its pages, and Kavita caught it carefully.
She turned it over in her hands as Osita slid some letters out of
the book and into his pocket without her noticing. "It's not
here," he said. Kavita looked up, disappointed, and set the
flower on the shelf.

"Are you sure?" Osita handed her the book. She looked through it slowly, then shook it, as if the pendant would burst out from the pages. "Isn't there somewhere else he could have kept it?"

Osita pretended to think, looking around the room again. The performance was depressing him, especially because he knew it would end badly for her. He walked over to the mattress and lifted it to check underneath.

"I already looked there," Kavita said. "Only some condoms."

Osita was glad she couldn't see his face. He went through the desk drawers as Kavita trailed behind him, her face growing sadder and sadder. "It's not here, is it?" she said finally.

Osita sighed. "I'm so sorry, Aunty Kavita. I don't think it is." Guilt filled him as she shook her head, dashing the edge of her hand against her eyes.

"It was like a part of him," she said, "and now it's gone and he's gone." She sniffled and looked up at her nephew, her face crumpling. "He's gone, Osita. I can't believe he's gone."

"I know, Aunty. I'm sorry." He hugged her in the humming silence of Vivek's empty room, holding her as she cried.

Down the corridor, Chika listened to his wife's swelling sobs, his phone beside him, lit up with missed calls. He didn't move from their bed.

Six

Vivek

I kept the book for the title, for how it was spelled. *Beautyful.* I had no idea why that spelling was chosen, but I liked it because it kept the beauty intact. It wasn't swallowed, killed off with an *i* to make a whole new word. It was solid; it was still there, so much of it that it couldn't fit into a new word, so much fullness. You got a better sense of exactly what was causing that fullness. Beauty.

Beauty.

I wanted to be as whole as that word.

Seven

Osita

I spent my last year of secondary school avoiding Vivek's house, not wanting to see his eyes or deal with the shattering in his voice. I didn't see Elizabeth either, but everything felt so spoiled with her; I couldn't imagine fixing it. I avoided the sports club, convinced she'd be there if I came, swimming slow laps in the pool or heading to the squash courts, her legs moving apart from my own.

My mother was quietly delighted that I was spending so much time at home. The deadlines to apply for universities abroad came and passed. Aunty Kavita might have reminded her, but the reminders never made their way to me. I wondered if I should follow up, but after my fight with Vivek, it felt easier to just let it go. I told myself that it had always been more of Aunty Kavita's dream, anyway. It was a strange thing for my mother and me to be accidentally united on—this idea of a foreign education dying like an unwatered plant in a dark corner. Instead I applied to universities in the country, those closer to home. Vivek's family had been selling us dreams I was no longer buying; my father was right, they were not my home.

Vivek came to my graduation with his parents. He and I acted like everything was fine when we met, but we avoided each other for the rest of the day. Before they left, Aunty Kavita came up to me.

"How come we haven't been seeing you around, beta? Did you hear back from the American schools? I sent your mother the application forms. You sent them in, yes?"

I had no idea what forms she was talking about; I'd never seen them. "Sorry, Aunty. I didn't get into any of the schools." I tried to look ashamed, which wasn't very difficult. "I was afraid you'd be disappointed in me."

"Oh, Osita!" Aunty Kavita hugged me tightly. "What are you going to do now?"

"I applied to some universities here just in case. Those ones went well. My father wants me to go to school in Nsukka."

She smiled and patted my cheek. "Well, at least you'll be close to home. Vivek is starting his applications soon. Fingers crossed for next year!"

My mother interrupted us, gathering the family to take a group picture. Her eyes met mine briefly, and I wondered how much she had overheard, how much she was hiding. I wasn't interested in digging up her secrets. We stood next to each other for the photograph; I still have it now. I'm wearing deep blue robes and looking sullen, a tassel hanging over my face.

Vivek isn't even looking at the camera. His eyes are cast off to the side and his chin is lowered. Aunty Kavita has her arm around his waist; she only reaches his shoulder. My father and uncle are standing next to each other, brother by brother. My mother is smiling so widely you can't help but look at her, like she's determined to crack her face in half. We fit easily in the frame, all of us together.

After I started attending university in Nsukka, my trips back to my home in Owerri grew less frequent. I didn't go to Ngwa either. A full year passed, maybe two, before I saw Vivek or his parents again. I wrote them letters, even called a few times after they installed a landline in their house, but I missed Vivek's graduation, his eighteenth and nineteenth birthdays, and it was only later I found out that he never went to America. No one told me why. According to my mother, he enrolled at Nnamdi Azikiwe instead. One term later, De Chika pulled him out—and still no one would tell me what was going on.

"Since when did you start caring about your cousin?" my father said when I asked. I flinched at the censure in his voice. He'd never commented on our rift, but clearly he'd noticed, and it sounded like he blamed me. I wanted to argue, but my father walked away without waiting for my answer, leaving me ashamed in his wake.

"Don't worry yourself," my mother said. "Focus on your books. The boy will be fine. His parents are just spoiling him."

"But what's happening?" I asked. "Why did they remove him from uni?"

She hesitated, then flapped her hand in a vague gesture. "He's not well, but don't worry. God will take care of it."

By then, my father had reduced his hours at work so he could spend more time at my grandmother's house in the village. "I'm getting old," he said, as if that explained everything, and maybe it did. The house had been renovated into a duplex and he'd put in a phone line. My mother and I joined him some weekends, like small holidays away from Owerri. The village was expansive—a world of land and farms and nature, not like the towns or cities, where everything was cramped and loud. We were finding escapes everywhere.

One evening at the village house, I picked up the phone in the upstairs parlor and heard De Chika speaking to my mother. I should have hung up, but instead I lowered myself to the floor next to the sofa, pressing my back against the leather and covering the mouthpiece with my hand so they wouldn't hear me breathing.

"You know Osita came down with us," my mother was saying. "Maybe it's a good time to bring Vivek around. You remember how close they were as boys."

"Mary, I don't know. I don't know what is happening to my son." De Chika sounded worried. "Do you know he stopped cutting his hair? If you see him now, just looking like a madman . . ."

"We will pray for him," my mother countered. "The forces of darkness will not triumph! No, he is not lost. He cannot be lost." I could already feel her beginning to whip herself up into a holy frenzy.

"I'm not worried about his soul, Mary," De Chika snapped.

"I'm worried about his mind. Kavita has stopped sleeping. She keeps checking his bed, but the boy doesn't even sleep there anymore. He wanders around the house. He goes and lies down on the veranda with the dogs. Sometimes he climbs the tree in the backyard and just stays there."

"Ah-ahn!" My mother was surprised enough to pause the spiritual momentum she'd been gathering. "Have you asked him what exactly he thinks he's doing? You can't just leave university to come and behave like this."

"He said he can't sleep. That the dogs don't disturb him and he can feel breeze better from the tree, some rubbish like that. When we asked him to start making sense, that's when he stopped talking. Mary, I don't want the neighbors to see him like this."

"Ei-yah! Poor Kavita. So it's the three of you that are coming, abi?"

"Yes oh. I can't leave either of them alone, and she won't leave him alone. You know she slapped him the other day?"

"Ehn, she told me. She said she was feeling guilty. I told her a boy who does not respect his mother enough to behave like a normal human being in her house should be prepared to accept some discipline. Didn't you people beat him as a child?"

"That was different. He was small, he was obedient. Kavita didn't tell you she was afraid?"

My mother perked up. "Afraid? Did he raise his hand to her?"

I flinched. She was wondering if he was like me. The last time she tried to slap me, I caught her wrist and forced her arm down. It was only through the veil of my anger that I finally saw the pain and fear in her eyes.

"Tufiakwa!" De Chika said. "How can? No, it's just the way he looked at her after she slapped him, as if he hated her. And I mean *really* hated her, from the bottom of his heart. And then the thing just went away, fiam! His eyes became as empty as a bucket—that's how she said it. She started crying and crying and he just continued looking at her."

My mother *tsk*ed over the phone. "Chai, you people are suffering! Oya, come and stay with us and maybe the air here will clear his head. You know that's why Osita likes to come also. He says everything is cleaner here than in Owerri, that the air is fresh."

"Ọdịnma. We will drive down tomorrow morning. Greet Ekene for me." De Chika hung up, then so did my mother and so did I. A few minutes later, she called me downstairs and assigned me a list of chores to prepare for their arrival.

That evening, we all sat around the dining table, eating garri and oha soup.

My father poured himself a glass of Guinness. "What time are they arriving tomorrow?"

"They said they will leave Ngwa early," my mother answered, spooning out more soup for him. "So unless they meet traffic, around nine a.m.?"

"Did you prepare the guest room for your aunty and uncle?" he asked me. "Your cousin will share your room with you."

I nodded. He glared briefly at me before turning to my mother to mutter something about how children of nowadays didn't know how to use their mouths and talk to their elders. I molded a ball of garri in my hand and thought about the last time Vivek and I had been in the village together. It was maybe five years ago, before the thing with Elizabeth, when he came back from his boarding school for Christmas. They had shaved his head while he was up there, and I joked that he looked like a refugee from Niger, one of those children always begging in the markets. We went to the river to swim, and when he took off his shirt, there were small round scars dotting his ribs. I asked him what happened, and he looked at me as if I wanted to fight him. Cigarettes, he said. From the senior boys. And then he jumped into the water and splashed me even though I was still dressed. We swam until my clothes dried on the banks.

Now, it felt like something that had never happened.

I went out running the next morning, before Vivek and his parents arrived. My shoes were filled with sand by the time I got back, so I emptied them outside the door, then entered the house in my socks. My parents were sitting in the parlor and my mother was holding Aunty Kavita's hands, praying quietly but urgently. De Chika was pouring a bottle of Star beer into a glass, even though it was still early. My father was drinking coffee. I bent my head and mouthed a greeting that De Chika acknowledged silently as he waved for me to move on. We all knew not to interrupt my mother's prayers.

I paused at my door, guessing that Vivek would already be

inside, and wondering if I should knock. A quick irritation flared through me: Wasn't this my own room, inside my own parents' house? Abeg. I opened the door and walked in, tossing my shoes into a corner loudly, steeling myself to see my cousin for the first time in years.

Vivek was sitting on my bed, and he turned his head when he heard me enter. At first, I couldn't even say anything. I just stared at him in shock, all thoughts of reclaiming my space gone. When De Chika said Vivek had stopped cutting his hair, I'd thought that highest, it would be touching his shoulders. It had always been curly, long enough to fall over his face—we used to joke that if he relaxed it, he would look like he was in a Sunsilk advertisement. He had De Chika's eyes and lips and hooked nose, even that reddish tinge under the dark gold of his skin, but his hair was as black as his mother's. Now it was below his shoulder blades, tangled, a little matted against the blue cotton of his shirt. He had lost weight and his neck seemed longer, his face balanced on top of it. His silver chain glinted out from under his collar, the small elephant lying against his skin. He smiled a little at the look on my face.

"Nna mehn, it's not as if I'm a masquerade. Stop looking at me like that."

"Have you seen yourself?" I shot back. "Are you even sure you're not a masquerade? Jesus Christ." I sat across from him and leaned my elbows on my knees. Clearly, something had seized my cousin. "Gwa m ihe mere," I said. "I want to know. I can see that you're not okay."

Vivek laughed. "You sound like my mother."

"I'm serious. This one that your parents brought you all the way to the village."

"You know your mother tried to pray over me already?"

"Deaconess Mary. What did you expect?" I peered closer at him. He looked so tired. "You haven't been sleeping."

"I see they're reporting me well," he answered. "I'm sure everyone has received the complete details." His lip curled as he spoke.

"Maybe my parents, but not me. I'd rather hear it from you anyway."

"Ah, Osita." He squeezed out a small smile. "It's a very long story."

I tried to smile back.

"You grew a beard," he said, reaching out to touch the tight coils on my face. I shrugged. I'd been shaving my head, the same way he used to, and the beard balanced it out. I liked the way my cheekbones cut above it, how dark my eyes looked. Vivek stroked my head, feeling the skin slide under his palm, still dappled with sweat from my run. "You know your father ordered me to either cut or wash my hair before I come back out?"

I snorted. "I wasn't going to even mention that one. You look homeless."

"I am homeless," he said, then shook his head. "Don't mind me. Can I take a bath, or do you need to go first? I can smell you from here."

I sucked my teeth at him. "I don't blame you. Biko, let me go first before you come and block the drain with all that your

Bollywood hair." He grinned at me and stood up when I did, stepping forward to give me a hug. He was almost my height, and smelled faintly of a spice I didn't recognize.

"Thank you," he said, as we thumped each other on the back.

"For what?"

"Not treating me the way they treat me."

My hands brushed against the tangle of his hair as we pulled apart. It felt soft. I stepped away from him and wiped my hands on my shorts. Vivek kept looking at me, but I couldn't meet his gaze directly. He was stranger than I was admitting to either of us, and it made me uncomfortable.

"Go and baff," he said, sitting down on the bed again.

I stepped away as if he'd given me permission to move, and once in the bathroom I locked the door. I used a bucket of water to wash myself, scrubbing and rinsing quickly, trying to get rid of the unsettled feeling that had entered me. When I came back out, with a towel wrapped around me, Vivek was still sitting on the bed, staring at the bars of the window in front of him, his back to me. I opened my wardrobe and got dressed. He didn't move. I stood for a moment before interrupting his aloneness. "Vivek. The bathroom is free."

He started and turned to me, some of his hair falling into his face. "Okay, bhai," he answered—brother, an old nickname he had for me. We were both our parents' only children, their only sons, more like brothers than cousins was the joke. It always made my chest tighten when he called me that. "Tell them I'm coming out soon," he added, dismissing me from the room. I nodded and closed the door behind me as I left.

My mother had laid out a late breakfast on the dining table, tins of Milo and Bournvita next to Nido milk and a flask of hot water, bread and guava jam—I knew Aunty Kavita had brought the jam, because she was the only one who ever made it—along with a bowl of boiled eggs, another full of akara.

"There's akamu on the stove," my mother said. "Go and help yourself."

Aunty Kavita hugged me. Even with her hair twisted up into a bun, she didn't reach my shoulder. "How is he?" she whispered.

"He's okay," I said. "He's washing his hair."

My father snorted and sat down, my mother fluttering over his shoulder as she put food on his plate. "He better be washing that hair. Chika, you should have made him cut it as soon as he entered your house."

De Chika shrugged and drew back a chair for Aunty Kavita. "What can I say, Ekene? It's not as if I could sit on him and shave it off by force."

"Then you should have thrown him out! What nonsense is that?"

"That's enough, Ekene." Aunty Kavita's voice was soft but firm. "He is my son, my only child. I am not turning him away, especially not when he's sick."

My father looked as if he was about to say something more, but my mother put her hand on his shoulder as she poured more coffee for him, and he subsided.

I went to the kitchen and spooned thick, glutinous akamu into my bowl, then went back to the table and added a layer of sugar. De Chika took the sugar bowl from me and added two teaspoons to his coffee. At least he wasn't drinking beer for breakfast anymore. I let my akamu cool off a bit—I liked it when it was a little congealed and starting to form a skin. For a while we ate together in silence, spoons clinking against bowls and coffee cups, until my father leaned over and turned on the radio, the new sound buzzing softly through the room.

"Amma!" Vivek's voice rang out from my room, and Aunty Kavita's head whipped up. Even De Chika looked mildly surprised to hear his son's voice. "Amma!" Vivek called again.

"Yes, beta?" she replied, already getting up from the table, her voice shaking a little. "What is it?"

"Can you come and help me with my hair?"

Aunty Kavita lit up at the request. "Of course, beta! I'm coming."

My father looked up from his plate. "Mary, you can lend her a pair of scissors, abi?"

Aunty Kavita glared at him as she left the room, and my father sighed. "It was worth a try. Walking around looking like a prophet. Ridiculous."

De Chika ignored him and unfolded a newspaper, a slice of bread and jam half eaten in front of him. I dipped akara into my bowl and ate it slowly. By the time I finished my breakfast, Vivek and his mother still hadn't come out of the bedroom. De Chika finally noticed and asked me to check on them.

This time I knocked. "Come in," called Aunty Kavita, and I pushed the door open. Vivek was sitting in the chair by the window and his mother was running a comb through his hair, now untangled and gleaming, draped over her wrist. He was holding an open container of coconut oil between his thighs and his eyes were half closed. "We've almost finished," she said. "It took a long time to comb it properly."

"I can imagine," I said. My aunt smiled absently.

"I always wanted a girl, you know. After Vivek. So I could do her hair."

"God works in mysterious ways," I joked, and she actually laughed.

"Not exactly," she said. "It's not as if I can plait his hair."

"You can plait it if you like," Vivek said, without raising his eyelids.

"Tch!" His mother smacked his shoulder. "Your father would kill me!" She resumed her combing, moving through his hair in slow waves. At this point she was just doing it for the sake of doing it. "No," she said, almost to herself. "We can't plait it. I'll just tie it back so it stops falling into your face. You know that drives your father crazy." She ran the comb through a few more times, then packed his hair into one hand, smoothing it back from his temples and forehead before securing it with an elastic band at the nape of his neck, twisting it into a clumsy bun. "Manage it like that," she said. "Your hair is so thick."

He tilted his head back and smiled at her. "Daalụ," he said, and she bent over to kiss his forehead.

"Come and eat some breakfast. Did you finish eating, Osita?"

"Yes, Aunty."

She brushed off Vivek's shirt as he stood up. "What do you want to eat, beta? There's bread, and I brought some of the jam you used to like, and Aunty Mary made akamu but we might have to heat that up again." He made a slight face at me as they left the room, his mother's voice washing solicitous over him. I made a face back to indicate he was on his own, then followed them into the parlor.

"I'm not hungry, Amma."

"No, you have to eat something. Let me heat up the akamu." She went into the kitchen and Vivek sat down, both of our fathers eyeing him.

"You look better like that," De Chika said. "With it tied back."

I laughed a little. "Ah-ahn, Dede, it's just hair." Vivek smiled but we both cleared our faces when my father lowered his newspaper to glare at us.

De Chika turned to me. "How is Nsukka?"

"It's going well. School is all right. "

"Your mother says you have a girlfriend there. You know, your father was your age when he got married."

"Don't mind that boy." My father's voice was derisive behind the pages of newsprint. "Play, play, play, that's the only thing he knows. No real responsibility."

"You have a girlfriend?" That was Vivek.

"It's not serious," I said.

"Your mother says it's serious," said De Chika.

"Chika, you and my wife gossip like old women." My father shook his head. "Shouldn't she be having those conversations with your wife?"

"Kavita doesn't find these topics interesting. I do. If you don't want to take an interest in your son's life, that's your own business." De Chika grinned at my father; he always took a particular pleasure in irritating his senior brother. My father rolled his eyes and returned to his newspaper, but I knew he was still listening.

Aunty Kavita came back into the room with a plate of akara. "Eat this, the akamu is warming." Vivek accepted the plate and started tearing the akara into little pieces, occasionally putting one into his mouth. His mother beamed at him and went back to the kitchen.

"So, is it serious?" Vivek asked.

I was starting to get annoyed. "It's none of your business," I said.

"You know I'll be your best man at the wedding. I think it's my business."

"That's a good point," De Chika said.

I could tell he was happy to see Vivek talking. I didn't want to ruin it. "I'm just getting to know her," I said. "That's all."

It was all a lie. There was no girl in Nsukka. I'd made her up on a call with my mother once, and her happiness was too great for me to deflate it with the truth. Instead, I pretended to be private about it so I could avoid the questions. It allowed her imagination to construct the perfect daughter-in-law, and I didn't have to talk about anything else; she could carry the whole conversation just based on that alone.

"What's her name?" asked Vivek.

"Jesus Christ, Vivek. Mind your own business!"

My mother shouted at me from the kitchen. "Osita! Did you just take the Lord's name in vain?!"

Vivek winked at me and I felt a surge of anger pierce through. "Sorry, Ma!" I called out, then I stood up. "I'm going out," I said.

"Your cousin is visiting and you're going out?" My father gave me one of his looks and I stared right back at him.

Vivek laughed. "It's fine, Dede. Let him go. I'm irritating him."

"Irri-what? My friend, if you don't sit back down!"

Aunty Kavita walked into the room and gave Vivek a bowl of akamu with a spoon suspended in it. "Actually, Ekene, do you mind if I send Osita to run some errands for me? Mary and I want to do some cooking later in the day."

My father glowered but allowed it, and I left the house with a shopping list and a chest full of relief.

At dinner, Vivek was subdued, eating his rice in small bites with his head bent. NEPA took light shortly after we ate, so I lit a kerosene lamp and went to my room to read a book. An hour later, Vivek came in, closing the door softly and kneeling beside the bed to light a mosquito coil. I kept my eyes on the page as the match rasped into fire, through the breath he released to extinguish it. The lamp made my book glow a dull orange that spread faintly to the walls. The rest of the room was halfway in shadows, swallowing Vivek in grayness as he pulled off his shirt and folded it, then took off his jeans and hung them in the wardrobe. I kept reading as he sprawled on the bed in his boxers and stared at the ceiling. Eventually his breathing settled. I put down the book and climbed into bed, leaning over to blow out the lamp. The room fell into black.

I listened to the crickets outside and the hum of our neighbor's generator. My eyes adjusted slowly, and I could see how the moonlight was coloring the inside of my room.

"So why did you lie?" asked Vivek, his voice close to my ear.

"About what?"

"The girl in Nsukka. There's no girl in Nsukka."

I scoffed. "Who told you?"

"Nobody had to tell me anything. You're a very bad liar."

I turned my head to look at him and his eyes were bright in the dark. "Mind your business, bhai."

His teeth gleamed in his smile. "The part I don't understand is why you're lying to them in the first place. You know your mother won't let it go until she's planning your wedding to this imaginary girl."

I looked back at the ceiling. "She's not imaginary," I said. I was already building her up. Her name would be Amaka. She'd be a nurse, or maybe a teacher.

"When you're hiding something," he said, "don't cover it up with something weak, something that can be blown away easily. You need to protect your secrets better."

I propped myself up on my elbows. "Bros, I'm seriously tired of hearing this nonsense. What secrets?"

"Maybe it's not a woman you're seeing in Nsukka," he said. "One of my friends at boarding school used to lie like you. He even had one of his classmates' sisters pretend to be his girlfriend." Vivek turned his head to me. "Do you have a backup girlfriend?"

I stared at him through the gray light.

"That's fine if you don't," he continued. "I'm just saying you need a better story."

"Wait." I felt as if my head was stuffed with surprise. "If it's not a woman, who else would I be seeing in Nsukka?"

Vivek looked at me, and there was a pause before I realized what he meant. I sat up, furious. "Are you mad? What's wrong with you?!"

I saw alarm flit through his eyes; he hadn't expected this anger from me.

"Ah, no vex," he said, sitting up and reaching for my arm.

I pulled away and jumped off the bed. "Don't touch me. You think I'm like your friends? Or like you? Is that why you decided to start looking like a woman, ehn? Because you've been knacking men? Biko, I'm not like you—forget that one, now-now!" I slapped the palms of my hands against each other, as if dusting off the contagion of his thoughts.

Vivek looked up at me, his back hunched and his legs lean and straight on the bedsheets. His hair had come loose from the bun and it spilled down his shoulders. "So you think I look like a woman?"

My chest was thudding. "What?"

"Is that why you avoided me all day? Because I resemble woman to you?" He laughed and pushed his hair back, off his chest. "You dey see breast?"

I shook my head. My stomach was knotted and painful. "You are really not okay. They should actually be praying for you."

"All of this because I said maybe you have a boyfriend instead of a girlfriend? It's not that serious."

"You think that's normal? You think you sef, that you're normal? None of this is normal, Vivek! What kind of people have you been around?"

"Why are you so afraid? Because something is different from what you know?" My cousin folded his arms and leaned his back against the headboard of the bed. "I'm disappointed, bhai. I didn't think you'd be one of these closed-minded people. Leave that for your mother."

"Fuck you," I said, and grabbed my pillow off the bed.

He laughed again. "Oh, you're going to sleep in the parlor? Let your mumsy find you there in the morning, then you can tell her why you didn't sleep in your room. Or I can tell her for you if you like."

I wanted to hit him. I felt like we were thirteen again, the way he was worming his way under my skin and making me want to itch it off. "I'm not one of those," I told him.

"One of what?" Vivek put up his hands. "Actually, never mind. I don't even care. I'm going to sleep. Do what you like." He lay back down, turning away from me.

I stood in the dark, holding my pillow and slowly feeling like an idiot. Finally I threw it back on the bed and lay down with my back to him. What a bastard. I lay there with the anger simmering in me for a long time before I fell asleep.

At some point in the night, NEPA came back and the ceiling fan whirred on. I stirred and woke up. I was lying on my back with an arm thrown out; Vivek was scattered beside me, his leg touching mine and his hair drowning my arm, the silver chain and pendant gleaming against his collarbone. I could almost see the lines that marked Ganesh. Vivek sighed and his eyes opened into slits.

"Sorry, bhai," he whispered, and drifted back to sleep. There was a tendril of hair lying on his cheek that I wanted to move aside, but I was too afraid to touch him. I lay still and looked at the ceiling until sleep collected me again.

Eight

Kavita thought it was a phase—that Vivek was just going through something and it would pass. So she prayed and said countless rosaries, rubbing the color off the beads with hundreds and hundreds of Hail Marys until she thought her hands were actually full of grace. She took him to the cathedral to see Father Obinna, the priest who had baptized him and fed him his First Communion. When Vivek came out from their conversation, his forehead was wet with holy water. "Pray some more," the priest told them, and Kavita believed him, trusted him. If there was something more, something spiritual, wouldn't the father have seen it? She wasn't sure. "The Catholic Church can't do anything," Mary told her over the phone. "You should allow him to come to Owerri, so I can take him to my own church. They fight these things with holy fire."

"I don't know," Kavita said. "He's been doing a little better since we got back from the village, you know? He's eating again, sleeping in his own bed."

"Has he cut that hair?"

"I don't think that's important—"

"Ahn! Kavita. You know how things are here. It's not safe for him to be walking around Ngwa looking that . . . feminine. If someone misunderstands, if they think he's a homosexual, what do you think is going to happen to him?"

Kavita's stomach dropped. The thought had worried her, too, but it was different—more terrifying—to hear it put into words. Vivek couldn't end up like those lynched bodies at the junction, blackened by fire and stiffened, large gashes from machetes showing old red flesh underneath. Most of them were thieves, or said to be thieves, but mobs don't listen, and they'd say anything afterward.

"He's going to be fine," she told Mary. "He was born here, raised here. People know who he is."

Mary laughed bitterly. "You think it matters? You don't know Nigeria. People have killed their neighbors and burned down their houses. He's not safe, I'm telling you."

Kavita started to get upset. "Why are you putting that into the world? Vivek isn't doing anything to anyone."

"I know it's hard to hear," Mary said, softening her voice. "But you know how these men are. The boy is slim, he has long hair—all it takes is one idiot thinking he's a woman from behind or something, then getting angry when he finds out that he's not. Because, if he's a boy, then what does it mean that the idiot was attracted to him? And those kinds of questions usually end up with someone getting hurt. Ekene doesn't want Chika to cut the boy's hair out of wickedness, you know. We're trying to look out for him. Just because he's half-caste doesn't mean he's going to get special treatment forever, not the way he's behaving. You're his mother. It's your job to protect him. I'm telling you, bring him to Owerri. We can help him at the church here."

"Let me talk to Chika about it," Kavita answered. It was an excuse she used when she wanted to end a discussion, pretending that she couldn't make a decision without her husband's input, and Mary, like everyone else, stopped bothering her as soon as she said it. They said good-bye, got off the phone, and Kavita went into the parlor, where Chika was reading a newspaper. "Your sister-in-law is getting on my nerves," she said, sitting in an armchair and crossing her legs, pushing her braid over her shoulder, the black of her hair now silvered with age. "She keeps trying to get me to bring Vivek to her church."

Chika didn't look up from his paper. "Mary means well," he said, his gold-rimmed glasses balancing on his nose.

"She said Vivek's not safe, that he looks—" She paused. "That people might try to hurt him." Her voice warped hesitant, unwilling to say out loud the possibility of worse.

Her husband sighed and dropped the newspaper into his lap before turning his head to her. "Well," he said, "is he?"

"Chika!"

"It's a fair question, Kavita. Look at how he presents himself."

"My God, it's just hair! It doesn't mean anything."

Chika gave her a gentle but knowing look. "Is it me you're trying to convince, or yourself?"

They stared at each other for a few seconds, then Kavita dropped her eyes. "What if it's something we did, Chika? What if we made a mistake somewhere and that's why he ended up like this?"

Chika reached out a hand and caressed her knee through the silk of her trousers. "Don't blame yourself," he said. "The boy has his own life, and we can't control every aspect of it."

Kavita nodded, pulling herself together. "You're right. Besides, he's getting better. He's even going out." She looked up at him. "Soon he'll be able to go back to school and everything will be normal again. You'll see."

Chika looked at his wife, at the hope thrumming out of her eyes, and said nothing. Kavita ignored whatever he wasn't saying. She knew he wanted the same thing for Vivek, so it didn't matter. He would see. Everything would be fine.

Vivek kept losing weight, so Kavita took him to a doctor, who checked his blood pressure and pulse, listened to his lungs, and asked him about his meals, frowning at his responses.

She put aside her notes and looked at Vivek, the collar of her white coat stark against her neck. "You know you're not eating enough," she scolded.

"I don't have an appetite," he replied, shrugging. "Everything tastes like nothing."

"You have to try," Kavita said. "Beta, I can see your ribs."

Vivek pulled his shirt back on and it hung from his shoulders. "I'll try, Amma. I promise."

"Are you smoking?" asked the doctor.

"Cigar or igbo?" Vivek quipped, and Kavita smacked his arm.

"Stop that nonsense."

The doctor just looked tired, or perhaps bored. "Either one," she said.

"No," said Vivek. He answered the remaining questions as Kavita gazed at his face, the smudged darkness around his eyes. They drew some blood for tests and the doctor told him again to eat some more before sending them away.

"Let me take him to my church," Mary insisted, when she called that evening to ask how the visit went. "It can't hurt, Kavita. They will try and remove any evil thing that has attached to him. You believe in prayer, I know you do. Your own church has not done anything for the boy. Let us try, biko."

Kavita was hesitant but she was, after all, his mother. She couldn't fold her hands and not try everything. So, that weekend, she sent him to Owerri. She'd wanted to wait and send him when Osita would be there but Mary advised against it. "That boy doesn't go to church," she said. "He'll just convince Vivek against it. We don't need another thing blocking his deliverance." So they didn't tell Osita that his cousin was visiting, and he wasn't there the weekend Mary took Vivek to her church.

Late Sunday evening, Kavita was in the parlor when Vivek returned from Owerri, slamming the mosquito-net door open as he came in. "Beta?" she called as he walked past the parlor. "How was it?"

Vivek stopped to look at her, and Kavita flinched. She

had never seen him so angry, fury just packed into his burning eyes.

"I'm never going to Owerri again," he said, his voice tight. "You people can go if you like, but I won't follow you. You hear?"

"What happened?" Kavita swallowed down the anxiety. Nothing could have happened. Mary would have called her if something had happened. "Was it the church service?"

Vivek stared at his mother. "Have you ever been to her church before?"

"Yes, of course, beta." She twisted her fingers together. "It goes on for a long time, but it seemed all right. What happened?"

"No, I mean have you ever gone when they're doing a deliverance?"

Kavita shook her head and her son leaned forward slightly, pinning her to the armchair with his unforgiving gaze. "But you sent me anyway."

She was starting to get alarmed. "Vivek, what happened?"

"They are bastards!" he spat. "You think it's all right to treat someone as if they're an animal? In the name of their useless deliverance? Mba, wait. They called it an exorcism. Because, apparently, I have *a demon* in me, did you know? They had to beat it out." He lifted up his shirt, revealing a swath of dark red welts on his side.

She gasped and stood up from her chair to go to him, but Vivek dropped the shirt and held out his hand, warning her away. "Don't touch me," he said. "And stop trying to fix me. Just stop. It's enough."

After that, Vivek locked himself in his room and didn't come out for the rest of the night. With trembling hands, Kavita picked up the phone and dialed Ekene's landline, rage biting inside her. She didn't understand. How could Mary have allowed them to do that to her son, to Mary's own nephew? "What is wrong with you?" she shouted when her sister-in-law picked up. "Ehn? Are you mad or what?"

"Kavita, gịnị mere?" Mary replied, sounding confused. "I've been trying to reach you all afternoon. Did Vivek reach safely?"

"'Did Vivek reach safely?'" Kavita repeated, mocking her voice. "Yes, he just got here—and he showed me what those bush people at your church did to him!"

"What?"

"My friend, stop pretending. I saw the welts on his body. You allowed them to flog him?"

"Kavita, I've been trying to reach you from since to tell you what happened. It's not him they were flogging, ịghọtala? It was the demon inside him."

Kavita stopped in shock. Mary couldn't be serious. "What did you just say?" she asked, hoping she'd heard wrong.

"The demon inside him," Mary repeated. "Yes o, that's what Pastor said. The boy is possessed by a very, very wicked spirit, a strong demon. It's what has been causing all of this, the long-hair thing, the wasting away of his physical body. Supernatural forces are feeding on him—on *your child!* Pastor said we must cut his hair because they are drawing their power from it, like the locks of Samson. This is one of the sources of their strength.

But when one of the deacons approached him with scissors, the demon started to fight back!"

Kavita listened in mounting disbelief. Surely this couldn't be the same Mary she'd known all these years? Impossible. She'd always been religious, but this was something different, something that smelled like rotten meat or madness.

"It wasn't your son," Mary continued blithely. "Pastor was saying it, and even everyone in the congregation, we could see it as well. It was the demon fighting to not lose its power. They tried to hold him, but he had the strength of many men. That's how you know it was the demon. No mortal man could have thrown off all the ushers who were trying to hold him. Eh hehn, so then Pastor said we must subdue the demon at all costs, and so we were praying and binding and casting it, and he brought out his cane to lash it, because you must lash it with holy fire and his own is like the staff of Moses—"

"Stop, stop, *stop.*" Kavita pressed her fingers to her forehead. "You're telling me you allowed this pastor to beat my son while you stood there and watched?"

"Kavita, you're not hearing me. *That was not your son.*" Mary was starting to sound irritated. "Should I just relax while the devil is using my nephew? I was praying with them, na! Praying for his deliverance, for his spirit to be purged of the evil overtaking it, but I'm telling you, the thing was too strong. He threw off the hands of the people holding him and he ran out of the church, piam! We tried to look for him at the house but he had already collected his things and left. That's why I've been trying to reach you, to make sure that he arrived home safely—because the deliverance was not complete. You and Chika must bring him back, ehn? Pastor says it is very crucial that we finish the deliverance, now that the demon knows we have exposed it. Time is of the essence."

Kavita pulled the receiver away from her face and stared at it as if its black plastic would help any of this make sense. As she put it slowly back to her ear, Mary's voice poured out again.

"Tomorrow if possible. Are you there? Are you hearing me?"

Kavita struggled to find the words. It felt like there was a stone in the back of her throat; she wanted to reach her fingers in, pull it out, and use it to bash in Mary's head, over and over. The feeling surprised her. "Don't come near my son again," she managed to choke out.

"Ehn? What did you say?"

"Don't *ever* come near my son again," Kavita repeated, her words clearer this time, sharper. She heard Mary's intake of breath as if the woman was standing behind her, but she would not stop. "You and your pastor are crazy. You stay away from my family, you hear? Otherwise I swear, I will show you pepper!" Kavita's hands were trembling again.

"Ah-ahn. You're talking like this to me? A whole me?"

"Before nko? Is there another Mary who went to church to go and abuse my son?"

"As I'm trying to help you and your son, this is how you want to treat me, ehn, Kavita? Out of the goodness of my heart I asked Pastor to help him, and this is how you're behaving? Do you know how many people beg Pastor to come and lay his hands on them? I even made extra offering on Vivek's behalf. Only to be rewarded with this your ingratitude." Mary sucked her teeth. "Why am I even wasting my time with you people?"

Kavita slammed the phone down, her skin itching. She wished Chika was home, but it was just her and her son. She went to the door of Vivek's room and stood there, staring at the wood. Of course he didn't want to talk to her, she thought, not after she'd sent him into that. Kavita sank to the floor and leaned her back against the wall, the linoleum cool under her feet. She pressed her forehead into her palms and cried.

Kavita didn't tell her husband what happened, not at first. Chika wasn't surprised by Vivek locking himself in his room; it was normal at this point, so he didn't ask any questions. Kavita, however, walked around with rage pounding through her, wondering how she could have failed to see what Mary had become, if it was her own carelessness that had resulted in Vivek getting hurt. There was no one she could talk to about it.

The next morning, Rhatha called her. The Nigerwives were convening an emergency meeting around Maja. "She just found out Charles has been keeping a second family," Rhatha told Kavita, her voice low and scandalized. "Can you imagine? Poor darling. We're all heading over there this afternoon."

The news briefly distracted Kavita from her own anger. "Is he still in the house?"

"Goodness, no. She kicked him out, and good for her! It's

one thing to have an affair, or even a mistress, but a whole family?" Rhatha clicked her tongue. "Are you going to come?"

"Yes. Yes, of course. I'll see you there." As soon as she hung up, Kavita grabbed her purse and left for Maja's house, though the meeting wouldn't begin for hours. Maja was her best friend; it was ridiculous that she was hearing this news through the grapevine—from Rhatha, of all people.

Maja burst into tears as soon as she opened her front door. Kavita dropped her purse, pulling her into a hug.

"Oh, my dear! Why didn't you tell me?"

"I'm—I'm sorry," Maja sobbed against her neck. "It's just—you have so much going on with Vivek, I didn't want to disturb you. . . ."

"Shh." Kavita stroked the woman's hair. "I'm here now. It's going to be okay." She pulled back and wiped the wetness off Maja's face. "Come sit down and you can tell me everything."

The story was even worse than Kavita had expected. Charles not only had another family, but his child with the other woman was a boy, his first and only son. And it wasn't just an affair: he wanted to marry the woman, to take a second wife.

"You can't mean it," Kavita said, aghast.

"He's serious." Maja dabbed at her eyes with a handkerchief. "He says I can't blame him, that no one would blame him for taking another wife when his first one has failed to give him a son. The woman's child is his namesake."

Kavita covered her mouth with her hand. "Oh, Maja, I'm so sorry!"

"He agreed to leave because I was making such a scene, but he says he'll be back, Kavita. He says he's going to bring the woman *into our house*. That I can't do anything about it. I told him I'd take Juju and leave, and he said I should try it." Tears tracked down her swollen cheeks. "I would leave, I really would, but I can't find our passports. I think he's hiding them. And I don't even know how to tell my parents, you know, because they warned me. They warned me African men were like this, and they told me it was foolish to come here with him, to bring Juju here. He said Juju is not enough, that she's not a boy. What if she heard him say that? As if she means nothing, as if she's nothing?"

Kavita held Maja's hand tightly. "Have you told her yet?"

"No!" Maja's voice was spiked and loud. She pulled it back down, shaking her head. "No, I can't tell her. I have to figure something else out. She can't know he did this, that he's like this. It would destroy her, and he's already caused enough damage. She thinks he's away on a business trip."

Kavita wasn't sure what to say. She didn't approve of secrets, but she also knew it was dangerous to tell another woman how to raise her child. She'd barely survived an argument in her own family when she and Chika decided not to tell Vivek that he was born on the same day that Ahunna died. The convergence had made his birthdays difficult—the way everyone kept trying to smile past the grief clotting inside them. They didn't want to tell Vivek because they didn't want him to think it was his fault they were always sad on his birthday, as if his arrival had caused her death. Kavita had thought the pain would fade over the years, but it had multiplied instead, like a load getting heavier and heavier on your head the longer you walked with it.

Finally, when Vivek was seven or eight, Ekene challenged them over it. "He deserves to know," he insisted. "This is his history, our family history. He needs to know what happened!"

"Is that so?" Kavita had folded her arms and glared at her brother-in-law. "How do you explain something like that to a child?"

Ekene fell silent.

Strangely, it was Mary who did it—Mary, before she became the woman she was now. She'd sat down with Vivek on her lap, his little legs kicking idly through the air, his hair dropping into his eyes. They hadn't started cutting it short yet, that came with secondary school.

"Your grandmother was a wonderful woman, Vivek," she told him. The boy didn't look at her, busying himself with a Hulk Hogan action figure he was turning over in his hands. "On the day you were born, she went up to Heaven and became an angel so she could look down on you and protect you."

He raised his eyes to her, with those long eyelashes. "She went to Heaven?"

"Yes, nkem. She went to Heaven on your birthday. So sometimes your mummy and daddy feel sad, because they miss her very much. You remember when you came to stay with us in Owerri for the first time and you missed your mummy and daddy and you were crying?" Vivek nodded. "Well, they feel like that sometimes, too. But they are also very happy because they got you, so it's a happy-sad feeling, you know?"

Bittersweet: that was the word for his birthday, though he was too young to know it then. Sweet on the tip of the tongue, sour and bitter notes scraping through the rest of the mouth.

Kavita and Chika got better at perfecting their smiles until he couldn't see through them; they pressed down their pain to protect him. What had changed? Nothing, really.

Kavita looked at Maja, who was doing the same thing, after all. Burying her hurt so her daughter wouldn't see it, trying to keep her safe. They were all trying to keep their children safe. She sat with her until the rest of the Nigerwives arrived, some bringing food because that's what they did, because it saved Maja the bother of having to cook for her family, or what was left of it. Kavita stood up and let them flock around Maja, hearing the story again, gasping and clucking and raining curses down on Charles, that useless bastard of a man. Kavita said nothing about Vivek and what had happened at the church in Owerri. It wasn't the time or the place, and besides, there was a tendril of shame unfurling into a leafy plant inside her. She was the one who had allowed Mary to do this to Vivek, when she should've known better. All the Nigerwives liked to make fun of what they called the fanatic Christians, always catching the Holy Ghost and convulsing on carpets, but Kavita had pretended they hadn't infected her family, as if she didn't know who Mary was. As if Mary was the same girl she'd known all those years ago when Ahunna was alive.

A sob caught in Kavita's throat. Ahunna would have known what to do about Vivek. She would've known exactly how to deal with Mary, what to say. Kavita took a deep breath and arranged her face properly. She had spent years learning how to push aside thoughts of Ahunna, of her uncle, thoughts that could paralyze her with grief. She had a child; she couldn't afford to fall apart. Chika had felt the same way, too, after Ahunna died, after the two of them nearly gave up on being parents and Ekene and Mary had to step in to help. "Never again," Chika had said, when the worst was over. "We can't self-destruct like this ever again. We have Vivek now. We have to be stronger." So Kavita was strong.

After another hour or two with Maja and the Nigerwives, Kavita went home and walked into the bedroom she shared with her husband. He was changing out of his work clothes, his white vest covering his chest and stomach. Kavita sat at the edge of the bed and told him what happened in Owerri, how Mary and her church members had beaten Vivek. She kept her hands folded in her lap and her voice level the whole time, even as Chika turned to her, a furious incredulity spreading over his face.

"She did *what?*"

Kavita tightened her jaw. "It was part of their deliverance nonsense."

"No, no. This has gone too far." Chika got up, hands on his waist, and paced the room. "You see? When I told Ekene that that church was corrupting her mind, did he listen? Of course not. He always thinks he knows what he's doing because he's the senior. Osita stopped coming home because of all that, and still, Ekene won't hear word. It has gone too far, you hear me?

He needs to control his wife! What kind of bush animals beat a young man in the house of God?"

Kavita took a deep breath and went over to her husband, resting her hands on his chest. "It's all right," she said. "I told Mary to stay away from us. We don't need that kind of nonsense in our lives. I've handled it."

Chika removed her hands, shaking his head. "I still have to talk to Ekene. Whatever happened between you women is between you, but my brother and I need to sort this out." He walked out of the room. Kavita watched him leave, then listened to his raised voice a few minutes later as he and his brother broke things even further. It was how he always did nowadays, pushing her aside gently, not listening to her. Sometimes it felt like he had stopped listening to her years ago, and she just hadn't noticed. Like they were living in two separate worlds that happened to be under the same roof, pressed against each other, but never spilling, never overlapping.

After Vivek died, their worlds drew even further apart. Chika didn't want to ask any questions. Kavita, though, was made of nothing but questions, hungry questions bending her into a shape that was starving for answers. They quarreled now, every day, from morning to night.

"Will it bring him back?!" Chika finally screamed at her one night, after dinner, standing in the kitchen. "All these your questions, what will they do? My son is dead!"

"Our son!!" Kavita screamed back, throwing a plate at him. He ducked and it shattered against the wall. "Our son! *Our son!*"

He had stared at her, then walked out of the room, but Kavita didn't care. She wasn't like him. She wasn't going to give up and sink into whatever trough of grief Chika wanted to fall apart and wallow in. Her questions were real. Who had returned Vivek's body to their door? Who stripped off her child's clothes, wrapped him in akwete, and delivered him like a parcel, like a gift, a bloody surprise? Who had broken his head?

It took the police several days to get around to making any kind of report. They blamed it on the riots that had happened the same day Vivek died, the market coughing black smoke over that side of town. "We had a lot of casualties there, Madam," the officer had said. "This is what happens when touts take over a town." He leaned back in his chair, his eyes bloodshot. "My condolences to you and your family. We will continue investigations."

"They won't continue anything," Chika said dully, as he and Kavita left the station. "Vivek was probably robbed."

"Then who brought his body home?" Kavita asked. "How did they know where we lived?"

Chika turned his flat eyes on her. "At least someone did. At least we have a body to bury."

He said it as if that was enough. As far as Kavita was concerned, that made him a liar, just like everyone else. Just like the police officer who told her weeks later that there was nothing more they could do for her. Just like Vivek's friends who kept telling her they didn't know what happened. It didn't make any sense. In those last few weeks of Vivek's life, his friends had been with him almost every day. Someone had to know something. They were just refusing to tell her. Kavita was sure of it.

She didn't care if all the Nigerwives thought she had gone crazy, because she wouldn't just bury her son and shut up. If it had happened to them, they would be behaving exactly the same way. They had no idea what it was like to know in your marrow that someone had an answer to your questions, that someone around you was lying. They had no idea how every breath for her was hell. She was going to find the truth, even if she had to rip it out of his friends' throats. Someone had to know what happened to Vivek.

Nine

Osita

I know what Aunty Kavita wants to know. I want to tell her that she is not prepared for the answer, the same way I was not prepared. That it will hit her like a lorry, spilling its load over her chest and crushing her. But I also know that I'm afraid of what she will find out, if someone will tell her what was happening, if Vivek told someone else what was happening.

If someone saw me that day.

Stop looking. I want to tell her to stop looking.

Ten

Vivek

I felt heavy my whole life.

I always thought that death would be the heaviest thing of all, but it wasn't, it really wasn't. Life was like being dragged through concrete in circles, wet and setting concrete that dried with each rotation of my unwilling body. As a child, I was light. It didn't matter too much; I slid through it, and maybe it even felt like a game, like I was just playing in mud, like nothing about that slipperiness would ever change, not really. But then I got bigger and it started drying on me and eventually I turned into an uneven block, chipping and sparking on the hard ground, tearing off into painful chunks.

I wanted to stay empty, like the eagle in the proverb, left to perch, my bones filled with air pockets, but heaviness found me and I couldn't do anything about it. I couldn't shake it off; I couldn't transform it, evaporate or melt it. It was distinct from me, but it hooked itself into my body like a parasite. I couldn't figure out if something was wrong with me or if this was just my life—if this was just how people felt, like concrete was dragging their flesh off their bones.

The fugues were short absences that I became grateful for, small mercies. Like finally getting to rest after having your eyelids forced open for days. I hid them from my parents and grew out my hair, thinking that the weight dropping from my head would lighten the one inside of me. It worked—not by making anything lighter, no, but by making me feel more balanced, like one weight was pulling the other and the strain on me had been lessened. Perhaps I had just become the fulcrum, the point on which everything hinged, the turning. I don't know. I just know that I hurt a little less with each inch of hair I refused to cut.

Looking back, I really don't know what I thought it was going to protect me from.

Eleven

Everyone knew that death entered with the upcoming elections. It was all anyone was talking about: if moving into civilian rule was a good idea, whether the military rulers could handle the country better. People argued in their homes and beer parlors; voices were raised, blows were thrown, and the violence sometimes escalated into bloody clashes on the roads. The day Chika brought Vivek home from university, they had run into traffic, cars crawling over potholes as people danced into the streets, whooping and singing.

Chika leaned out of his window, irritated. "What's all this?" he shouted at a boy who was crossing in front of the car, waving palm fronds and holding a bottle of malt in his other hand, brown foam spilling over his knuckles.

The boy turned to him with a broad smile, his teeth catching sunlight.

"Abacha don die!" he shouted back. "Abacha don die!" He

dipped between two cars, narrowly missed being hit by an okada, and was lost in the growing press of people.

Chika pulled back into the car and a hesitant smile spread over his face.

"Thank God," he murmured, and Vivek, who had been sleeping with his head thrown against the car seat, woke up and stared blearily around him. His hair was damp with sweat from the back of his neck. The collar of his T-shirt was darkened with it, as was the fabric under his arms.

"What's happening?" he asked.

"Abacha is dead," his father replied, swerving the car into the next lane and cutting in front of a bus. The driver shouted and made rude gestures.

"So what happens now?" Vivek asked.

"It's a new day for Nigeria," Chika replied. "A new day." He smiled at his son and put a hand on his shoulder. "For all of us."

Perhaps he was right and it was a birth of sorts, but Chika had forgotten that births come with blood, and in the case of his son, they came with loss as well, birthdays and deathdays all tangled up in each other.

A few weeks into Vivek's return, as tensions arose between the police and a vigilante group, a seven o'clock curfew was imposed in Ngwa. Vivek had been taking long walks at night, and when his parents told him he'd have to stop, he lost his temper. "You're keeping me in a cage!" he shouted. "You think I want to stay in this house every night like a prisoner? Is that why you brought me back?" He ran outside and refused to come back in after it got dark. He climbed the plumeria tree in their back-yard, cradling himself in its broad branches.

"Leave him there," Chika said, disgusted. "Let him fall out and break his neck. Onye ara."

He slammed the back door behind him and refused to let Kavita go outside so she could beg Vivek to come indoors. "Beg him for what? I said let him sleep there with the chickens!"

In the morning, Vivek was covered in mosquito bites and there was a splatter of yellowwhite chicken shit on his shoulder. After Chika left for work, Kavita boiled water for the boy to take a bath. She didn't know what to say to him, so she said nothing. While he was bathing, she called Rhatha and invited her to come over with her daughters.

"It'll be good for the boy to have some company closer to his age," Kavita said. Rhatha brought her signature cupcakes, complete with sugar dragonflies perched on top of the icing.

Somto and Olunne came in matching blue jeans with floral cutouts and garish polyester blouses with draping sleeves. They smelled like bubblegum, and their hair was pulled tight into ponytails.

"You girls have gotten so big!" said Kavita, as they hugged her hello. "I'm sure Vivek won't even recognize you. How many years since you last saw him? Four? Five?"

Somto brushed an imaginary crumb off her green blouse and smiled at Kavita. "Closer to six or seven years, Aunty. Before we left for boarding school."

"Yes, yes, that's right. Well, come in, let me go and call Vivek."

"It's okay, we remember where his room is," Somto said. "Can we go and give him some cupcakes?" She looked at her mother first, then at Kavita for permission. Olunne's eyes widened at her sister asking to go into a boy's room, just by themselves, but she rallied and gave Kavita a quick smile, a shy flash of teeth.

Kavita and Rhatha exchanged glances, then smiled back at the girls. "Down the corridor," said Kavita, and watched as they traipsed off with the tray of covered cupcakes.

"That's friendly of them," she noted.

Rhatha waved a hand. "Oh, they heard he's got such long hair now and wanted to see it for themselves. I think they're halfway jealous."

Kavita blinked. "Over hair?"

"Darling, you wouldn't believe it. They're obsessed with those Sunsilk advertisements and they quarrel over whose hair is longer all the time. It's ridiculous."

"Oh, that's right, they had to cut their hair for school, didn't they?"

"Yes, but it didn't kill them." Rhatha flapped a hand and sat next to Kavita, her face solicitous. "But tell me, darling, how are you? You must be worried sick about Vivek."

Kavita suppressed a sigh. Rhatha was a bit of a gossip, always spilling people's business. If she hadn't been one of the few whose children were around, Kavita might not even have asked her over. She wondered what rumors Rhatha had heard. "He's doing all right," she said. "We just wanted to give him a little break from school since he hasn't been feeling well."

Rhatha leaned back in the sofa and regarded her. "You know," she said, "Eloise was at the glass factory the other day when Vivek came to pick up Chika. She said he was looking quite run-down. It must have been serious if you pulled him out of school."

Kavita frowned. "Why was Eloise at the factory?"

"She was picking up some sculptures. You know they did that program recently with the local artists, for her children's ward? Their work is quite ugly, if you ask me, dreadful vases and whatnot. Chika was holding one for her. He didn't tell you?"

"Yes, I remember," lied Kavita. "Of course, the sculpture."

"You should take Vivek to the teaching hospital if you need to get him checked out. Eloise is there a few times a week."

"I know. But he's fine, really. He just needs some time. He was always sensitive, even as a child."

Rhatha nodded knowingly. "Nerves," she said. "You always have to watch the sensitive ones. They wear out so easily, and the last thing you want is a nervous breakdown."

"Exactly," agreed Kavita. "Better he have some time off now than break down at school." She knew there was a chance Rhatha would run around and tell everyone Vivek was on the verge of a nervous breakdown, but it was better than admitting that the breakdown had already happened.

"I thought that military school would have toughened him up," said Rhatha.

"That's what Chika was hoping when he sent him," replied Kavita, unable to keep the bitterness out of her voice. The other

Nigerwives knew the whole story—she'd vented to them about it years ago when Chika first made the decision, despite Kavita's objection that the boy was too young to live so far away from them.

To her surprise, the Nigerwives had supported Chika. "You have to allow him to raise his son the way he wants to," they said. "We're overprotective because this isn't our country, but Chika knows what he's doing. You trusted him enough to stay here instead of going back home, so trust him with your son." So Kavita did; yet every holiday she waited with a tight chest until her son was back in her arms, safe and browned from the harsh sun.

"I hear it's so hot there you can use the water from the tap to make garri?" she'd asked him, during one of his first holidays back home.

Vivek had laughed. "Yes, Amma. It's Jos. You can grow strawberries up there."

She had been worried that he'd be targeted for being Igbo, but her neighbor Osinachi had laughed when she heard that. "He looks Hausa," she said. "Or even Fulani. He will be fine there. The boy doesn't even hear Igbo like that." Osinachi was an architect whose husband worked in Kuwait. She had lost her oldest child in a car accident years ago, and their surviving son, Tobechukwu, had grown up to be—as Osinachi put it—a bit of a tout, a troublemaker.

"Kavita?" Her mind had been drifting, but Rhatha's voice drew her back.

"Sorry," she said.

"I was saying that maybe the military school idea wasn't the best. He might have had to repress his natural sensitivity, so it's breaking out now."

Kavita barely stopped herself from rolling her eyes. "How are your girls?" she asked instead, and Rhatha preened. The only thing she loved more than prying into other people's lives was talking about her two darlings. She went off on a glowing monologue about how wonderfully the girls were doing with this time off, how they were exploring their artistic sides, how Somto's swimming was bordering on extraordinary. Kavita smiled and nodded, tuning out most of Rhatha's words. They had some tea and biscuits, and after an hour or two the girls came out of Vivek's room carrying a tray still full of cupcakes.

"We should have baked something else," Olunne said. "I forgot he doesn't like these."

"Isn't he coming out?" asked Kavita, making to stand up.

"No, Aunty," said Somto. "He got very tired and he said he's going to sleep for a while. But we had a nice time. Thank you." She put the cupcakes on a side table. The mothers were expecting them to say more about Vivek, but it was as if somewhere within the walls of Vivek's room, allegiances had shifted, unseen pacts had been made, and Somto and Olunne had stepped out carrying Vivek's secrets in the elastic of their ponytails. It was clear they had no intention of sharing what had happened, so everyone sat awkwardly in the parlor for a bit until Rhatha took the girls home.

Later that night, when Vivek came out for dinner, the table was tense. Chika was chewing his cowtail with aggressive crunches and Kavita could hear her cutlery ringing against her plate.

"How was it having some friends over?" she asked Vivek.

He looked up from his food and his face was calmer than it had been since he returned home. "It was nice," he said. "Thank you for inviting them." His voice was level and polite, and Chika glanced at him in surprise. After dinner, Vivek excused himself, washed the plates, then went to bed.

"What happened to that one?" asked Chika.

"I think he just needed some friends," Kavita said. "He can't be isolated all the time; it's not good for him."

"Aren't those girls much younger than him?"

"Only by three or four years, Chika, come on. They played together all the time as children."

"They're not really children anymore," he noted, unfolding a newspaper, and Kavita swatted him on the arm.

"Shut up," she said. "He's a good boy." She didn't ask Chika about Eloise's visit to the factory. She didn't care.

"I still think we should take him to the village this weekend," Chika said. "I talked to Mary about it. Osita will be there."

"Oh, good! I haven't seen that boy in so long."

So that was how they came to take Vivek to the village house. Kavita combed his hair, and when they returned to Ngwa, Vivek started going out to visit Somto and Olunne more and more. If he stayed out past curfew, he just ended up spending the night at Rhatha's house. His parents didn't mind; they knew he was safe there, and the boy seemed to be doing better, so they were happy.

One day, Kavita called Rhatha's house to check on Vivek. "The boy isn't here," Rhatha said in her high and lilting voice. A spike of panic shot through Kavita's chest.

"What do you mean, he's not there? He hasn't come home yet."

"Oh, no, he's fine. They're over at Maja's house."

Kavita frowned. "Really? Why?"

Rhatha paused. "She does have a daughter their age, darling."

"Oh my God, yes, of course. I just . . . I didn't know the children were friends."

"I don't think they liked the girl very much when they were younger—Juju, that's her name, yes? Well. They're all as thick as thieves now." Kavita could almost hear Rhatha shrug over the phone. "Children and their politics. Who can understand it?"

Kavita laughed and got off the phone as quickly as possible, so she could call her friend.

Maja picked up almost immediately. "Yes, the children have been coming here," she told Kavita, holding her phone to her ear with her shoulder as she rolled white stockings off her legs. "Rhatha's girls, Vivek, even Ruby's girl, Elizabeth. They all go to Juju's room to watch movies and play music and whatever else they get up to."

"It's strange that they're suddenly so close," Kavita said, and Maja laughed.

"It's cute," she said. "It's just like when they were little."

"You don't think they're . . . you know, up to something in there?"

Maja paused as she unhooked the clasp of her uniform skirt. "Really, Kavita? Like what?"

"I don't know! Smoking or something. Drinking?"

Maja exhaled. She tried to be patient with Kavita, she really did, considering the fact that Vivek was clearly having some kind of breakdown, but there were lines. "So you think they'd just be doing all that in our houses and none of us would notice? Because we're what, that negligent with the children?"

"Ah, no, that's not what I meant."

"Kavita, stop being so neurotic, for goodness' sake. The children are fine. They're on holiday, and they're staying indoors instead of being out there with all this wahala going on. Did you hear about the attack down on Ezekiel Street?"

"What? There was an attack?"

"Yes, the day before yesterday. The clinic there—armed robbers, they're saying."

"During that riot?"

"Mm-hmm. They broke the electric signboard, someone threw a stone at it, and later that night those robbers came back and attacked the clinic."

"Jesus. What's there to steal from a clinic?"

"Ask me. They think all these barren women overpay because they're so desperate for children. I don't know why they think there'd be any money there. Most of these patients just end up owing the doctors anyway." She paused, then, more quietly: "I heard they raped some of the nurses."

"My God, Maja."

"Ruby was telling me about it. I'm tired of this country,

Kavita. Brutality everywhere. I'm thinking of taking Juju and going."

"I thought you said Charles hid your passports."

Maja shrugged, even though Kavita couldn't see her, and started unbuttoning her shirt. "And so? I will find them somehow. Or go to the embassy and make a complaint. What am I staying here for, after the way Charles has treated me? Let me swallow my pride and ask my parents for help."

"Will you go back to the Philippines?"

"I don't even know." Maja leaned against the wall, her shirt falling open. She was alone in her and Charles's bedroom. They had told Juju he was away on a business trip, and he was, handling it all from a hotel in Onitsha. Maja wasn't sure if he had taken his other family along with him. "Where else would we go?" Her voice was deflated.

"I'm so sorry, Maja," said Kavita. She knew that Maja wouldn't leave Charles, not really. She was too afraid of him, too in love with him, too stubborn to admit that her marriage wasn't what she kept telling her parents it was. Charles knew it, too. He'd spent years whispering into Maja's ear that she would never make it on her own, just her and Juju, that they needed him, that her daughter needed a father.

"Where are you going to go?" he'd said. "You know the kind of shame it will bring to your family if you don't have a husband. It's better you stay here and make it work, adapt to our customs. Welcome my second wife when she comes. Behave with some dignity and don't embarrass me. It will be good for Juju to have a little brother in the house." When Maja tried to argue back, he smiled patiently and twisted her wrist till it bruised. "I will give you some time," he said. "I believe a family should live together. You hear? But I will give you some time."

Maja wished she was like Tammy, whose husband had done the same thing, gone and taken a second wife, except that Tammy had given him sons already. The man thought Tammy would ignore it, because he was rich and she and their children lived in a gorgeous house with lavish grounds. Instead, he'd come home one day to find the house empty and his children gone. Tammy took them back to Scotland and that was the end of it. She didn't even shout. The other Nigerwives told that story with pride, but Maja knew her story wasn't going to end like that. Charles had already warned her that he would come and find her wherever she went, so if she wanted to run, she had better leave his daughter behind. Maja didn't quite understand why Juju meant so little, yet so much to him. Like property.

"I have to go," she said to Kavita. "I have to make dinner for all these visitors."

"Send them back to their houses," laughed Kavita. "As if they don't have food there."

"I don't mind. It's nice to have them around, you know? The girls are turning into lovely young women."

"And I'm sure Vivek is enjoying himself with them," added Kavita. Part of her was hoping that he was like other boys— that he actually *was* up to something behind closed doors with the girls. She couldn't contemplate another option.

"You know, sometimes I forget that he's not one of the girls," said Maja.

Kavita pressed her lips together and kept the annoyance out of her voice. "Of course. What with that hair. Let me let you go and handle them."

She put the phone down. She's only saying that because she's jealous, she thought. Because her husband is ruining her life. Because she doesn't have a son.

Meanwhile, up Agbai Road, Chika watched as Eloise scrambled up from her knees in his office, her cheeks flushed and red. She was smiling as she wiped her mouth, a smile that puzzled and annoyed him, as vacantly good-natured as if she'd just passed him the salt at dinner. He tucked himself back into his trousers and zipped them up, watching her adjust her blouse to cover her breasts.

"Do you think Kavita knows?" she asked, cutting a mischievous look at him.

"You're her friend," he said pointedly. "What do you think?"

Eloise pulled a brush out of her bag and used her reflection in a glass cabinet door to brush her hair into order. A few minutes ago, his hands had been clenched there, messing it up. "I thought maybe Rhatha said something to her after I ran into her the other day."

Chika shook his head. "Kavita didn't say anything."

Eloise paused. "Well. That's odd. I'm sure Rhatha would have told her. Why do you think she didn't bring it up with you?"

"I don't care," he said. All he really cared about was getting Eloise out of his office. Of all the Nigerwives, she was the one he disliked the most—for how loud and brash she was at her parties, for the nondescript blandness of her face, for the fact that she even did this with him at all. The others would never. She has no morals, Chika thought; God knows what else she's been doing under her husband's nose, with none of her children there to occupy her. He hated himself a little for getting involved with her, but Kavita was so preoccupied with Vivek. He was the only thing she wanted to talk about, day or night. She all but dragged the boy into their bed, running her theories past Chika on what was wrong with him and how he could get better, droning into his ear and waving him away when he tried to touch her. Vivek was his son and he loved him, but Kavita was taking it to another level. Their marriage was suffering, yet their son was all she could see.

And that was how Eloise had entered the story. She'd been doing some consulting for his factory while their company doctor was traveling, so he'd asked her to lunch and she brought him some cake she'd made from home. Next thing Chika knew, he was kissing her thin lips and she was allowing it; then he was bending her over his desk like it was a dream, watching himself sink into her, her large pale buttocks rippling under his advances, his hand covering her mouth to keep her quiet. He'd just needed some relief, he told himself at home that night, his wife chattering away beside him in bed, still as beautiful as the rose garden. Chika reached for her, wanting to wipe away his memory of that afternoon, but she'd swatted his hands away.

"Are you even listening to me?" she said. "I still don't think the boy is eating enough. He moves the food around his plate as if I'm not going to notice. . . ."

Chika flopped on his back and let her words drain around him. A few days later, when Eloise brought him a bit of short-bread, he closed the office door and did it again.

His coworkers pretended not to notice what was going on. He liked that Eloise didn't even try to pretend to care about his family life. She never mentioned Vivek. She just brought whatever she'd baked, then unbuttoned her blouse or hiked up her skirt or opened her mouth or all of the above. She didn't expect tenderness or small talk, and Chika was relieved because he had neither to offer. In fact, he liked being rough with her, see-ing the blood rush up under her blued skin when he slapped it, sending her home with small marks and half hoping her hus-band would find out.

Would Kavita even notice if he came back with lovebites covering his neck? he wondered. The more he thought about it, the angrier he grew. He started asking Eloise to come by, started meeting her in hotels, even once met her at her house when her husband was at work. That one was too much for him, though—seeing the pictures of their sons on the shelves, smelling the man's cologne. He fucked her in the parlor, wiped himself on her dress, and left.

A fter Maja got off the phone with Kavita, she fed the chil-dren dinner and told Vivek to walk Somto and Olunne to the main road so they could get home before the curfew. They caught an okada and left, turning to wave at him. Vivek waved back, then dropped his arm to his side. The evening was cool and he knew he should go home, but the air was clear so he decided to take a walk.

He stopped at a kiosk near where the okada drivers gathered and spent ten naira on two packets of Speedy biscuits. One he tucked into his pocket and the other he ripped open, crunching them into his mouth. His slippers dragged over the ground as he strolled, and a few people cast quick looks at him. His hair flowed off his head in waves now, past his collar and down his back, but his shorts and T-shirt were clean and untorn, so he looked a little normal at least.

He walked past the new Mr. Biggs store that had opened just a month before, now filled with people buying their meat pies and sausage rolls. A girl with bright blue eye shadow and shiny lip gloss was sitting at the window, holding an ice cream cone—chocolate and vanilla soft-serve swirled together and curving into a point at the top. She licked it with singular focus, and Vivek wondered why she was alone. He walked past the building, past the banks next to it, up until he reached the supermarket. He pocketed the packet of biscuits and stepped inside. He needed to pick up some Nasco wafers to replace the chocolate ones Juju had finished when she came to his house last week. Maybe this time he'd go for strawberry or vanilla— she didn't like those as much and would leave them alone.

Vivek wandered through the aisles, goods stacked heavily on either side of him, cartons up to the ceiling. There were packets of dried beans, lengths of stockfish, boxes of cornflakes, sacks of rice. Vivek pulled the wafers from the biscuit shelves, next to the Digestive and Rich Tea biscuits. As he pulled his money out from under the biscuits jammed into his pocket, he heard a commotion outside, voices raised and shouting. He looked up to see a few people running past; others had stopped outside, staring toward where the runners were coming from.

Vivek thanked the cashier and took his wafers, then came outside and looked down the road. A small mob had gathered a few blocks down, too far away for him to see exactly what was going on. The girl from Mr. Biggs hurried past him, eye shadow shining on her scared face.

"Wait! What happened?" he asked, stepping into her path.

She flicked her eyes at him impatiently. "They're saying that they've caught a thief. They're going to take him down to the junction."

A young boy holding a tire—it looked as heavy as he was—ran past them, shouting excitedly, his body jerking as he lugged the weight down the road. Another boy followed him, holding a small jerry-can in each hand. They had no covers, so when the liquid sloshed out of them and spilled on the ground, Vivek could smell the sharpness of the petrol. The girl flagged down an okada and pushed past him to hop on it. She didn't look back as the motorcycle roared down the road away from the noise and people. He stood and watched, adrenaline surging through him. He didn't know what he was waiting for. As the mob drew closer, the road cleared, onlookers scrambling into nearby shops to get out of the way. Vivek stood where he was, feeling as if things were draining out of him. The cashier from the supermarket poked her head out of the door.

"My friend, pụọ n'ụzọ!" she shouted, waving at him to get out of the way.

Vivek didn't hear her. People had spilled into the road and cars were diverting impatiently. A taxi pulled up next to Vivek, brakes screeching, and a young man jumped out. He slapped Vivek hard on the back of his head. Vivek reeled as the guy grabbed him and dragged him toward the taxi.

"Tobechukwu?" he said.

Their neighbor's son glared at him. "Sharrap and enter this car," he said. "Useless idiot." He shoved Vivek into the backseat and climbed in after him, slamming the door. "Oya, dey go!" he shouted at the driver, and the car pulled away. Vivek twisted to stare out of the back window and Tobechukwu hit his arm. "Face your front!"

Vivek stared at him. "What are you doing?"

The mob receded behind them and Tobechukwu sucked his teeth loudly, stretching the sound to show his contempt. Clumps of his beard stuck out from his clenched jaw. They rode back to their street, where Tobechukwu pushed Vivek out of the car. He paid the taxi driver, and when Vivek tried to thank him, Tobechukwu glared at him.

"Go home to your mother," he said, "and make sure you don't tell her how stupid you were today." He walked into his compound, the metal of the gate clanking behind him.

Vivek stood in front of the gate for a few minutes, wondering what would have happened if he'd been swallowed by the mob. Would he have run with them down to the junction, just to see what it was like to be part of a whole? Or if someone had

seen him for what he was immediately, a piece that didn't match
anything else, would they have just thrown out an arm to remove him from the road, maybe pushing him into a gutter?
Why had Tobechukwu stopped for him? They barely spoke to
each other, not since their secondary school fights, even after all
these years of growing up with only a fence between them.

Vivek slid his hand through the bars of the gate and maneu-
vered the padlock on the inside bolt. Both his parents were in
their room when he entered the house.

"Vivek? Beta, is that you?" Kavita called out.

"Yes, Amma," he replied.

"Is it not after curfew?" said his father, looking up from
his book.

Vivek looked at the clock. "Only five minutes," he called
back.

"There's food in the kitchen," his mother said.

Lowering her voice, she added to Chika, "At least he's home
and he's safe."

"For how long?" replied Chika.

His wife patted his arm. "Relax," she said.

Kavita changed into her nightgown. Together, she and
Chika listened to the small sounds of Vivek in the kitchen—his
footsteps into his room, the click of his door.

Outside, smoke rose from the junction, but it was swallowed by the night.

Twelve

Vivek

The girls dragged me out. I don't think they meant to. I knew my mother was behind their visit; it was one of the few times a plan of hers actually worked.

I was drowning. Not quickly, not enough for panic, but a slow and inexorable sinking, when you know where you're going to end up, so you stop fighting and you wait for it to all be over. I had looked for ways to break out of it—sleeping outside, trying to tap life from other things, from the bright rambunctiousness of the dogs, from the air at the top of the plumeria tree—but none of it had really made any difference. So I was giving up; I had decided to give up. That afternoon, Somto and Olunne burst into my room and spoiled my whole plan.

They knocked first, but I ignored it. Then they knocked again and I heard a flutter of quick conversation before one of them turned the handle and opened the door. It would have been Somto; she always made the decisions because she was older, because she was never afraid. I sat up in bed as they came in, in time to see Olunne close the door, a slight sorry across her face. I'd drawn the curtains, but Somto switched on the light. She looked at me, shirtless in pyjama trousers, lying in bed in the middle of the afternoon.

"So," she said, tilting her head so her ponytail swung behind her shoulders. "What's wrong with you?" Her sister nudged her but Somto ignored it.

I blinked at the intrusion of the light. "Many things," I said.

"I can see that," said Somto, making a face. She put the cupcakes on my desk and plopped herself on my bed. "You look terrible."

I drew back with a frown. They were acting entirely too familiar, entering my room and sitting on my bed as if they knew me. Whatever had happened a childhood ago didn't make us friends now; we hadn't even seen each other since secondary school. Olunne glanced at her sister, then sat on the bed with me.

"I think you look pretty," she said, and that surprised me enough to knock the frown off my face.

"What?" I said.

Olunne reached out and pulled at my hair gently, just enough to make it stretch and spring back, then touched her fingers to the silver Ganesh I wore around my neck. "I said, I think you look pretty. Your hair is beautiful. You've lost too much weight—that's why Somto is saying you look bad. But you don't, not really."

I looked from one of them to the other.

"You must be tired of them talking about you," Olunne added.

"Everyone is talking about you," her sister said. "They're saying you've gone mad."

"Yet here you are, entering my room to talk about it," I snapped.

Somto shrugged. "I think there's probably something more interesting going on," she said. "Why not just come and ask you?"

"It's none of your business," I said. I didn't know why their kindness was making me so spiky.

Olunne put a hand on my knee. "Don't mind her," she said. "You don't have to tell us anything if you don't want. We just thought that maybe, if you felt like talking, it would be nice to have someone who was ready to listen. Actually listen. Not like how they like to say they're listening."

Somto scoffed in agreement.

I was, I must admit, taken aback. Alone is a feeling you can get used to, and it's hard to believe in a better alternative. Besides, it was true that all of us used to be friends, even though it was years ago, when we and our lives were simpler. And now they were being nicer to me than anyone had bothered to be in a while, so I tried to relax.

"Are those cupcakes?" I asked, and Olunne smiled, hopping off the bed to get the tray. I picked up one and peeled back the wrapper, biting into it mostly out of politeness. True to form, it was sickly-sweet, as Aunty Rhatha's cupcakes always were. "Jesus," I said, making a face.

Somto swiped a fingerful of icing from another and licked it. "You don't have to eat the whole thing," she said. "She still hasn't learned how to put a normal amount of sugar in them."

I put the cupcake down and shook my head. "I can feel my teeth rotting already."

Olunne leaned over and picked the sugar dragonfly off the cupcake, popping it into her mouth. That was how we found each other again, in a blocked-off room filled with yellowing light: two bubblegum fairies there to drag me out of my cave, carrying oversweet wands. I don't know how deep I would have sunk if not for them. I wish I'd told them more often how much that mattered to me.

I wish I'd told Tobechukwu, too, how often I thought about how he stepped in for me. We'd fought a lot when we were younger, but that was nothing special: I fought with almost everyone because I was slim and some suspicion of delicacy clung to me and it made boys aggressive, for whatever reason. Some people can't see softness without wanting to hurt it. But after I came back, after growing out my hair, Tobechukwu didn't react like other guys in the area did—calling out insults and sometimes hurling empty bottles my way so they could laugh and watch me dance to avoid the spray of broken glass. It couldn't be because we were neighbors, because our mothers liked to have tea together. Aunty Osinachi always came, brought some biscuits, stayed for about forty-five minutes chatting, then left, but this hadn't stopped me and Tobechukwu from fighting back when we were in secondary school.

I didn't understand him, not until one night when he

showed up at the boys' quarters, where I was smoking out on the landing, and sat down next to me.

"I can smell that from over the fence," he said, and held out his hand. I passed the joint to him and watched him hiss in a long, crackling breath. He handed it back to me as he exhaled, smoke spinning out of his mouth in a thin swirl.

"It's your first time dropping by," I noted, and Tobechukwu nodded without saying anything. We sat there in silence for a while until I turned to him.

"Why?" I asked. I wasn't sure what exactly I meant. Why was he there? Why had he helped me that day? Why hadn't he come before? I didn't know which question I was asking or which one he thought I was asking. But he didn't answer; he just turned his head and watched me pull in another smoked-up breath, watched me exhale and pass the joint back to him.

He stood up and stepped in front of me, tilting his head back as he inhaled. The moonlight fell over his throat and I could smell the old salt of his sweat. He handed it back to me and my fingers brushed against his, my head buzzing from the high. He blew the smoke down into my face gently, looking at me with a careful blankness. I realized how close he was standing to me, the proximity of his thighs under his cargo shorts, the subtle forward thrust of his hips. I smiled to myself and set the joint aside on the milk tin cover I'd been using as an ashtray. Hunger radiated the same everywhere, throbbing and loud even without words. I didn't mind it.

Tobechukwu didn't stop me when I reached for the waist of

his shorts and unbuttoned them, leaving his belt on. In fact, he adjusted his legs a little so I could reach in and pull him out, heavy and long against my palm, soft and smooth. I looked up at him and saw him watching me with a cool curiosity, his arms hanging relaxed by his sides. He reminded me of the senior boys from when I was in boarding school, their complete assurance that it was well and right for me to provide them with pleasure, an assurance so solid that nothing they did shook up who they believed themselves to be: boys who could not be broken, boys who broke other boys and were no less for it. The difference was that Tobechukwu seemed indifferent, not threatening. If I stood and walked away, I knew he wouldn't stop me, but I didn't want to leave. He waited and his pulse beat along my palm. He only closed his eyes when I took him into my mouth, his hand sliding to the back of my head, fingers caressing my hair, tangling in it. So this was why: he liked how I looked, he'd come to see if he was right about me, and he was. I sank my fingers into the backs of his thighs and he tugged at my hair, groaning softly in the back of his throat as he slipped into the back of mine. He felt like a stranger. He felt perfect.

After a few minutes he pulled away, trailing saliva from my teeth. He was still soft. I watched him tuck it in and zip up, then reach for the stub of the joint and take a final hit before stubbing it out on the concrete.

"Thanks," he said, then walked away as if nothing had happened. I stared at his back, and in one beat I was alone again in the boys' quarters, the taste of his skin still inside my cheek, the moon above, and desire reverberating emptily in me. I laughed. I couldn't help it—there was nothing else to do. Everything had stopped making sense a long time ago. I lay back on the concrete and let the mosquitoes eat me up in a thousand little love-bites, feeling so terribly lonely. At least, I thought, he and I were even now.

Thirteen

Osita

My mother gave up on De Chika and his family. She was convinced Vivek was possessed by something that would take them all down, and us too if we allowed it.

"I have told Kavita that she should bring the boy back for deliverance, but she doesn't want to hear." Her voice rang harsh with condemnation. "Leave them."

It was hard to watch, the way she severed her love for them. When I finally decided to pay them a visit, it was easy not to tell my mother. I wasn't sure about my decision; it was months after we were all at the village house together, and I hadn't spoken to them since. Still, when Aunty Kavita opened their back door, she didn't seem surprised to see me.

"Vivek's not here," she said, hugging me.

I kissed her cheek. "He's not?" I'd been expecting to find

him shuttered away, playing the recluse that he was in my imagination.

"He's probably at Maja's house, visiting Juju." Aunty Kavita smelled like lemongrass and curry. She wiped her hands on her skirt and smiled at me. "You remember their house, right?"

"Of course," I said. "Make sure you save me some curry, they don't feed me at home." Her laughter floated behind the screen door as it drifted shut.

It was the start of the dry season; the air was clear and sharp as I walked down the street to Juju's house. Aunty Maja's gate was unlocked, so I pushed it open and walked through the garden, up to their front door, and rang the doorbell.

Juju opened it, and I stared. She'd braided her hair, and the tails hung over her bare shoulders, brushing against the pink dress she had on—she looked nothing like the lanky, unfriendly girl I'd known growing up. I could see glimmers of her mother in her face now, hiding in the clear dark honey of her skin.

"Hey," I said, and she stared.

"What are you doing here?"

"Just like that?" I joked. "You can't even say hello?" We hadn't seen each other in years. She smiled and kissed my cheek, but the smile was halfway and the kiss was perfunctory. "I wasn't expecting you, that's all."

"Nsogbu adịghị." I brushed my cheek against hers, doubling the greeting. "I'm just looking for Vivek."

Juju's face closed up. "Oh. Actually—"

I raised a hand to stop her from having to come up with a lie. "I just want to see him, Juju. He's my cousin."

She exhaled heavily and stared at me. "I have to check," she said. "Wait here." The door closed behind her, leaving me out on the veranda, staring at her mother's cattail flowers. A tight knot of anxiety crept up between my shoulder blades. I'd been trying so hard to not think about why I was there, why I was trying to see Vivek. I knew the reason—of course I knew—but to admit it was more than I could handle. I had to pretend, otherwise I would turn and walk back through the hibiscus-lined path and out of that gate and drive back to Owerri and never come back. So I counted the cattails to keep me from running away. I'd reached fifteen when Juju opened the door.

"He said it's fine," she told me, stepping aside to allow me in.

"But you don't agree," I said, watching her face.

At first Juju didn't reply, simply leading me upstairs to one of the bedrooms. At the door, though, she paused. "I don't even know why he wants to see you after the things you said to him in the village," she said. "But if he says it's fine, I suppose it's fine."

My face heated in shame. "He told you about that?"

Juju's stare didn't waver. "Yeah, he did. And he's different now, Osita, very different. So be careful. If you're going to say something like what you said before, it's better that you just go home now, ịnụkwa?"

"I'm not going to say anything like that, I swear. I just . . . I need to see him. I want to know if he's okay."

She stepped aside, still watching me, and as I turned the door handle, she put a hand on my arm. "I'm asking you. Take it easy."

"I hear you. I'm not going to do anything." I pushed open the door and closed it behind me, Juju hovering on the other side as the wood clicked shut into the door frame.

Vivek was standing at the window, leaning against the wall, his fingers curled softly around the iron bar of the window protector. I sucked in a quick draft of air, my heart thudding against its own membrane. My cousin had lost even more weight; his hair was down to his waist. I stared at his wrists, his slender ankles, the white caftan he was wearing. Vivek turned his head as he heard me enter, and I saw both the bruised shadows under his eyes and the soft red of a lip tint staining his mouth. He didn't move.

"Osita," he said, and his voice was a stream of memory, my oldest friend. Seeing him hurt my chest. He looked as if he was dying. "Juju said you would look different," I said.

Vivek smiled. "I look worse, I know. Don't worry, I've just been sick. But I'm getting better."

"Okay," I said. "And . . . the lipstick?" There was no point pretending I didn't see it. He lifted a shoulder, then dropped it, indifferent. He was watching me, curious to see how I would react. "You know it makes you look—"

Vivek laughed. "It makes me look like what, bhai? Like a fag? Like a woman?"

I waved a hand, embarrassed. "No, no, that's not what I meant. I was going to say it makes you look different, that's all." Even me, I wasn't sure if I was lying. I wasn't sure what I thought. My cousin folded his arms and smirked, which annoyed me. "Come on," I said. "It's not as if I would lie to you."

"How's that your girlfriend?" Vivek asked, pushing some of his hair behind his ear. I flinched, and he smiled. "You know, the one in Nsukka. You never managed to tell me her name."

There was something different about him, and it had nothing to do with how he looked on the outside. It was something more insidious, something coiled in his eyes that I'd never seen before. For the first time, I felt afraid around him. It didn't feel like I was standing in a room with my cousin, with the man who was as close as I was ever going to get to a brother. Instead it felt like I'd fallen into the orbit of a stranger, like I'd stumbled across worlds and now I was here, out of breath and off balance.

"There's no girlfriend," I said. In the face of my confusion, I fell back on the truth.

Vivek lifted his chin, mild triumph flashing in his eyes. "Okay," he said. "Does it feel good to not lie anymore?"

I frowned. There was an undercurrent in his voice that I didn't like. "Are you angry with me?" I asked him. He huffed and looked away, walking to the bed and sitting on it, his bare feet against the patterned carpet.

"I don't know. Maybe." Vivek threw his hands up and let them fall against the sheets. "Fuck. Yes." He looked at me and his eyes were holes in his face. "I'm angry with you because you abandoned me, you know? You just . . . threw me away."

I flashed on Vivek, sitting on the landing of the boys' quarters, teary and apologetic as I walked away. "We were children," I said, the words weak.

My cousin laughed. "We haven't been children in a long

time. I didn't hear pim from you after the village. I thought you would reach out after that."

The room was heavy and silent. He wasn't making any accusations, not yet, but I could feel them anyway, like pinpricks against my skin. "I didn't mean to just disappear," I said, but then my voice trailed off.

"Well, it felt like you didn't want to see me. I thought maybe you were disgusted."

"Vivek . . ."

"You sounded disgusted by me." A corner of his mouth twisted. "Trust me, I know what that sounds like coming from you. I've heard it before." The way I'd looked at him after the incident with Elizabeth: he was right, I'd been disgusted then, but only because I had lost Elizabeth.

"I'm sorry," I told him. "It wasn't your fault, what happened at the boys' quarters. You couldn't control what was going on with you."

"That sorry is late," Vivek replied. "I don't need it anymore. I know it wasn't my fault."

He sighed and looked at me. "Why did you come here? What do you want?"

Now I was ashamed. I hadn't come to see if he was okay; I'd come because I needed him, and it was only now dawning on me how incredibly selfish that was. "I'm an idiot," I said out loud. "You're right, I shouldn't have come here." I began to turn away, but Vivek stood up.

"Wait, wait. I didn't say that. Seriously, I want to know. Why did you come?"

I didn't turn back to him. It was easier to tell the story if I wasn't looking at him, if I was looking at the wall and the window, the trees outside it. "It's stupid," I said, and was horrified to feel tears sharp behind my eyes. "It doesn't matter."

"Osita." Vivek's voice was a ruler, flat and hard. "Tell me."

So I told him, my voice unstable and small: About the small, dark club I'd been in the previous weekend, the young university student who leaned in to kiss me in a smoky corner, and the way I allowed it, allowed him even though anyone could look and see us; allowed his tongue to push into my mouth, even kissing him back before I came to my senses and pushed him away and left. About how he tried to talk to me about it the next day, bright-faced and eager, how panicked I felt because I didn't know what he thought I could give him, what world he thought we lived in where it was safe to do something like that. About how I lied when he brought it up, claiming I couldn't remember what happened, blaming it on whatever we'd been drinking. About the way his face collapsed in hurt and a fresh aloneness.

"You were the only person I could tell," I said to Vivek, looking down at my hands. "So I came here."

He was silent for a moment. "Why did you need to tell anyone?" he asked, finally. "Why didn't you just keep it a secret? Isn't that what everyone does?"

I opened my mouth to answer, then closed it again because I didn't know how to explain it—the thing that the kiss had exhumed in me, the way it was loud, the way it wouldn't be quiet. I had to do something, to give it room to unfurl, and Vivek was the only place I felt safe.

"So that's why you came here?" he continued. "Are you ashamed? You don't want to be like that?"

I scoffed, still not turning to look at him. "How am I supposed to answer that? You want me to stand here and tell you that I don't want to be like you?"

Vivek's voice turned cold. "If it's true, why not say it? What's your own? You didn't have a problem saying it before."

I kept quiet.

"Do you even know what I'm like?" His voice was shadowed with contempt now; he was disgusted by me. "In fact, forget that one. You came here so that—what?—I can make you feel better about yourself? Even after how you treated me, so I can tell you, Oh don't worry, Osita, it's okay to be like that?" His voice came closer but I kept my eyes on the wall. Vivek shoved me in the middle of my back. "Is that why you came? So I can *fix it for you?*"

He pushed me again and I stumbled forward, catching myself against the glass of the window. I couldn't avoid him; there was nowhere to go, so I turned to face him. My cousin was furious. His eyes were hard and glittering, his mouth was tight. I could understand his anger—after the things I had said to him in the village, for me to come and admit that in the end I was exactly what I'd denied, it must have felt like a betrayal. I had kicked at him, only to come crawling back, asking him to see me. I thought about backpedaling, I could claim the boy at the club had been mistaken, but it was too late: both of us would know I was lying, and as much as Vivek would despise me for it, I would hate myself even more.

"You have no shame," Vivek spat. "What do you want from me?"

I used to know the answer to that. I had just wanted to talk to someone who would understand, but now, faced with him and the fatigue bracketing his mouth, I shocked myself. I watched my hand wrap around his wrist, my fingerprints marking his skin as I surged forward and kissed him so hard that my teeth knocked against his, the way I'd wanted to ever since I'd seen him sitting on my bed at my parents' house, since I'd woken up that night with his hair on my arm and his body so close to mine. Vivek's pupils flared as my other hand knotted behind his head. He hit my chest with his free hand, trying to get away, but I couldn't let him go. Our eyes were locked, two swirling panics, and he wrenched his face away. I was still holding the back of his head and his wrist.

"What are you doing? What are you doing?"

His voice was shaking. I should have let him go—I should have let him go, but I didn't.

"I don't know." My breath was falling on his face, he was so close. I couldn't look away. His eyes flickered, picking apart the fear in mine. "I don't know," I said again. I was starting to get very afraid of the line I'd just crossed. I slowly released his wrist and slid that hand past his ear, into his hair, cupping his head with both hands. It felt as if hot ants were skittering under my skin, all over my body. I tried not to think of how humiliated I was about to be, when he would step away, when he would look at me with a fresh disgust. I held his head so he couldn't move, not yet—I was stronger than he was—and lowered my mouth to his again. I don't know why; I hadn't intended any of this, planned any of it.

I kissed him like I wanted to seduce uncertainty away, slow and gentle, filling my mouth with a plea and pouring it into his. He smelled like grass and wind and clothes that had been dried in the sun. Gradually, I felt him relax and relief overwhelmed me. His mouth softened under mine and then he was kissing me back, his hand like a dropped flower against my chest, petal-light and trembling as if there was a breeze. I stopped the kiss and released his head, dropping my hands to my sides. He could leave if he wanted, he could go.

Vivek stood with his hand still on my chest, his breathing uneven. His head was down, black curls falling onto the embroidered neckline of his caftan, against silver thread. He seemed to be thinking, so I stood still, looking down at him, waiting for him to decide. I deliberately kept my mind empty, except for him, because I knew as soon as I started to think again, I might go mad from what I had just done.

Moments passed. Vivek said nothing; his thoughts were slipping along some invisible course, too far away from me. I braced myself, then slid my right hand along the front of his trousers. My fingers grazed across taut fabric and he gasped, looking up at me in shock. I was relieved to find him so ready, to know that it wasn't just me. He whispered my name and I stared at him without moving. I took my left hand and pulled his palm to me, pressing it against my jeans so he could feel how hard I was, how much it hurt. My cousin shuddered and leaned into me, into my hand and against me, and my entire body became one loud thrill.

"You see?" I whispered. I had no idea what I was talking about, just desire maybe, but he nodded like it made sense.

"Okay," he said, and stepped away from me. "Okay."

Vivek walked across the room and covered his face with his hands, dragging the skin down. "Can we just lie down for one minute? I need to lie down."

"Of course." I tried to sound calm.

"Okay. Thank you." He climbed onto the bed and lay on his back, draping his forearms over his eyes. I hesitated before I lay down next to him, then stared at the ceiling. I could hear him beside me, taking long deliberate breaths. He was trying to calm down.

"Is this real?" he asked.

I knew exactly what he meant. It felt as if we had stepped out of everything we knew before and into something else entirely, as if what had just happened couldn't have happened on the other side, only on this side.

"Yes and no," I answered, my voice hesitant. "Whatever you want."

Vivek turned his head and uncovered his eyes to look at me. "Have you done this before?"

I almost laughed. It was such a far cry from those days when he was the virgin and I was the one who made fun of him. Now it was as if I was starting over, as if I didn't know anything.

"No," I admitted. "Never. Have you?"

His gaze didn't waver. "Yes."

I was surprised at the pang that shot through me. "Oh. Okay."

Vivek rolled over on his side and put his hand on my cheek, turning my face to him. "Are you jealous?" He sounded amused.

"Fuck you," I said, and he laughed at me.

"You're jealous," he sang, then he kissed me and pulled up my shirt, touching my stomach, dipping into my jeans. "Don't be jealous," he whispered, as his fingers drew me out. My body bent up to the ceiling and Vivek lowered his head till his hair was a shadow spilling across my hips.

I died at his mouth.

It was the clearest terror and pleasure I had ever known. How was it possible that the boy who once chipped my tooth was the same one with his cheek now pressed against my navel? I could feel the shame like a shadow in my chest, but it was faint, insignificant. I didn't care. I didn't care. I would do it again, all of it, for him, always for him. I clutched at his head and cried out as I came, my whole body a naked wire. Vivek pulled himself back up and wrapped his arms around me. I couldn't stop shaking.

"Hey, hey." He tightened his hold on me. "Osita, it's all right. It's all right. Just breathe."

My fingers were clawed in the fabric of his caftan and every muscle in my body felt locked. He touched his forehead to mine, and his skin was cool. "Bhai," he whispered. "Relax."

For some reason, I wanted to hit him. I couldn't tell if he was comforting or restraining me, but his strength was much more than I'd expected. I could barely move in his hold. How stupid I had been, to assume that I'd been the one restraining him earlier, the strong one. He had stayed in my hands because he wanted to, not because I was making him. How stupid I had been, full stop. I struggled, but he wouldn't release me.

"Let go," he ordered, and I felt my throat twist, sounds choked within it. "I'm here. It's all right. Let go, bhai." My face was pressed into his chest and when the scream made it out of my mouth, it sank against his body, the volume muffled. I was sobbing—stupid, embarrassing sobs—and Vivek put his mouth to the top of my head. "You're safe," he murmured. "It's just me. It's just you and me."

We lay together like that until all the tears had wrung their way out of me, until we both fell asleep, wet with each other's salt.

Fourteen

Vivek

If I didn't love Osita already, I would have for that evening alone. For coming to find me, for kissing sense into me. For breaking himself apart, trusting me with his secret.

Later that night, I woke up to him unhurriedly kissing my neck. He was gentle as he pulled up white handfuls of my caftan, gentle when he touched me with spit-wettened hands, when he entered me—you would have thought it was my first time, not his.

The sheets dragged in fractions beneath us. I turned my head to look back at him. "I'm not going to break, you know."

Osita rocked inside me slowly. "I know."

"I'm serious." It was hard to think with that much of his skin all around me. "You don't have to take it easy."

He pushed deeper, one glorious inch at a time, and I groaned. "I know," he said, his voice thick. "Just take this for now."

I know what they say about men who allow other men to penetrate them. Ugly things; ugly words. Calling them women, as if that's supposed to be ugly, too.

I'd heard it since secondary school, and I knew what that night was supposed to make me. Less than a man—something disgusting, something weak and shameful. But if that pleasure was supposed to stop me from being a man, then fine. They could have it. I'd take the blinding light of his touch, the blessed peace of having him so close, and I would stop being a man.

I was never one to begin with, anyway.

Fifteen

Juju knew nothing about her half brother until she saw him with her own two eyes.

She'd been all the way over by the post office, which was two buses away from home and heavily crowded thanks to the fish market across the road. Maja had warned Juju never to take an okada there—people drove so recklessly, it wasn't safe—so when Juju got off the bus, she walked the rest of the way to the post office, dodging speeding motorbikes and tiptoeing along the edge of rank gutters. The air smelled like dead seawater.

Juju was on her way to swap out some of her books and see if she could find something for Elizabeth at the open-air secondhand-book market that happened every Saturday at the post office. "Check if they have any Pacesetters," Elizabeth had said. She and Juju were in a new relationship, hiding it from all their parents, and Juju had been feeling guilty about not being present enough. She was fairly sure that her father was having an affair and that her parents weren't telling her about it, which didn't make sense because the secret was too big, too loud. Her mother was always whispering on the phone, then shouting at her father, when they thought Juju was asleep. Her father's voice would scorch through the night and Juju would hear the familiar thuds of his hands hitting her mother. She was surprised when he actually left—it looked too much like him letting her mother win, and Juju knew him better than that—but she was glad he was gone, glad that the air in their house was calm and they could move a bit more freely. But between her new relationship and what was happening with Vivek, Juju had been distracted. This was her first time dating a girl, and it was easier, in some ways, to focus on other things rather than on Elizabeth and the terrifying feelings Juju had about her. Still, she wanted to get Elizabeth the books. She could at least do that one as her girlfriend.

Juju was looking through the five Pacesetters she'd managed to find, feeling victorious, when she glanced up and saw her father. She fumbled and dropped one of the books, pages fluttering in panic. Charles was standing next to a short woman with wide hips and an auburn weave-on. He was holding the hand of a young boy, maybe five or six. The child resembled Charles so strongly that Juju immediately knew what she was looking at: her father's other family. She stepped back, merging into the people around her, disappearing. He was supposed to be in Onitsha, she thought. For business. Yet here he was, in their own town, with this woman and this little boy.

Her first thought was to rush home and tell her mother. She'd already started pushing through the crowd, toward the bus stop, when a sick feeling hit her stomach: her mother already knew. No wonder he'd left. He had a whole other family to go home to, and he didn't even have to leave town to reach them. Juju glanced back at her father and saw the woman smiling up at him, her teeth shining like a Colgate advertisement. That gleaming joy made Juju want to take a stone and smash it into the woman's face.

Just the other day she'd pressed herself against the bathroom door and watched her mother cry soundlessly while pulling out a discolored molar from her own mouth with a pair of small pliers. Maja's jaw had been swollen for a while—she'd told Juju it was from an infection, which was true, but it was also from a fight with Charles. She hid the bruising with makeup.

"Mama, why don't you go and see a dentist?" Juju had asked, wincing as she watched the tooth clatter into the sink.

Her mother gargled with peroxide, spitting a swirl of foam and blood. "You have to travel to see a good dentist. Sometimes even overseas."

"So why don't you travel?"

Maja's eyes glittered with the anger she usually hid from her daughter. "Why don't you ask your father? Tell him all my teeth are rotting in my head!" She pushed past Juju and slammed her bedroom door, leaving her daughter wavering behind her.

Now, looking at her father in the market, Juju felt a wave of revulsion so strong it made her want to bend over the gutter and vomit everything she'd eaten that day. She wanted to kill him; maybe she would, if he ever came back home. Poison his soup or something. It couldn't be that hard, and no one could tell her he didn't deserve it, not with her mother's broken heart, not with her bloody tooth left in the sink.

Juju went home and threw the books in a corner of her room, then climbed into bed and listened to her pulse as it galloped through her. She was too angry to cry, too young to save her mother and take her away from this country and the man who had trapped her here. She covered her face with a pillow and screamed into it, and that was when the sobbing started, large and loud, stopping only when she had cried herself into an exhausted sleep.

Juju woke up to a faint knocking from downstairs, the sound winding up the stairs in an insistent thread. She groaned and rolled out of bed, then went down to open the door. Vivek was standing outside in jeans and a green T-shirt with butterflies scattered over the front. The word *Philippines* was embroidered in cursive underneath. Juju recognized the shirt—her mother had passed it over to Vivek after her father refused to wear it. ("We're in Nigeria," he'd said. "No one is interested in your country.")

Vivek walked past Juju into the house. Someone had plaited his hair for him and it hung like a snake between his shoulder blades. "Were you sleeping?" he asked. "It's still afternoon."

Juju closed the door behind him. "I took a nap." Her head felt stuffed and heavy. Vivek jogged up the stairs to her room and Juju followed, watching as he spun and landed on her bed.

"Wow," she said, "you really have energy today."

He eyed her up and down. "Unlike some of us," he retorted. "What's disturbing you?"

Juju shook her head. The pain was still too personal, the information too new. Juju wanted to hold it, cup it in her hands a while longer before she uncurled her fingers to expose it to others. She sat on the bed next to Vivek, then flopped back, staring at the ceiling. "Do you think I'm a bad girlfriend?" she asked.

Vivek turned to her, lying on his side and propping up his head with one hand. "To Elizabeth? Why would you think that?"

"I don't know." Juju twisted the end of one of her braids between her fingers. "I don't know if I'm doing it right." She hadn't planned any of this; she hadn't grown up with a crush on Elizabeth, not the way Osita had. Juju had been reluctant to make friends with the Nigerwives' children, because she didn't believe in ready-made communities—you couldn't just throw people together and expect them to become a real support system simply because they had one or two things in common. Their mothers might have been able to do it, but that's because they were a proper organization. It didn't mean their children had to follow suit.

But then Vivek came home, and Somto and Olunne showed up for him, and when they brought him to Juju's house she'd fallen for him, in a way—not like she fell for Elizabeth later, but she and Vivek had clicked. They fit into each other's lonely worlds. Everyone could see it; even Somto and Olunne didn't mind seeing him and Juju grow close so quickly, maybe because as sisters they'd always known what it was like to have a best friend. For Juju it was new; for Vivek, she thought the friendship might have taken some of the sting out of Osita's absence. But now Osita was back, and now Juju had Elizabeth. She still couldn't believe she had a girlfriend—hurtled into each other's lives thanks to the Nigerwives, who apparently never grew tired of shoving their children at one another.

It wasn't as if Maja and Ruby had meant for their daughters to fall in love, or even knew anything about it. All they'd done was start a jam-making experiment. They had a whole list of jams they were going to make: guava, mango, pawpaw jam. Maybe even some marmalade. Maja had dragged Juju into it, buying a bag of large green guavas—the kind Juju liked, crunchy and white on the inside. But Ruby suggested it might be better to make it with the other kind of guavas, the small, soft ones with pink or yellow insides, so Maja had sent Juju to Ruby's house to collect a bag of them. "We'll try it both ways and see which one works better."

Juju had rolled her eyes, but she loved her mother and the jam experiment was fun, so she went. That was the day she met Elizabeth again, and the thing Juju always remembered about it, that day, was the heat. How it pressed down through the air, wet and insistent, how it forced its way past skin until it felt like even your bones were hot. Juju caught a bus that was almost full, and sat on the conductor's fold-out seat, the backs of her thighs sticking to the torn vinyl seat cover. The conductor was squatting by the open door, holding on to the frame of the bus as it sputtered down the road. Juju leaned away from the woman next to her, who stank of stockfish and sweat. The heat was cooking the stench, deepening it till it was overpowering, almost choking. By the time Juju reached Aunty Ruby's house, she was fanning out the hem of her T-shirt to try and get a breeze against her skin. Aunty Ruby's gate wasn't locked, so Juju walked into the compound and straight to the back door. It was open, but the mosquito-net door was closed and latched.

"Hello?" she called, wiping her forehead. "Is anyone around?"

Footsteps came down the corridor; then Elizabeth appeared, hazy behind the green mesh of the mosquito net. She was wearing shorts and a singlet, as tall as she'd ever been. Juju stood with a polite smile as Elizabeth unlatched the door.

"Good afternoon," she said, wincing a little at how formal she sounded. "I'm Aunty Maja's daughter?"

Elizabeth stared at her for a moment, her face blank, and Juju stared right back. She remembered Elizabeth's face, but back then Elizabeth had been a lanky, dark-skinned child with threaded hair and puffy dresses. Now she had shaved off her hair, and Juju felt herself staring at all that skin, from her scalp to her arms and legs, even the smooth cleavage that the singlet couldn't quite cover. She wasn't wearing a bra. Juju blushed.

"Oh, Aunty Maja," Elizabeth finally said, after a forever of staring silence. Her voice was deep and sweet. "You're Juju. Come in." She moved aside to make space and Juju tried to walk through the doorway, but it was impossible to do so without brushing against Elizabeth, who didn't move. She just smiled and looked down as Juju squeezed past. "It's nice to meet you," she said, and Juju wondered if she heard a trace of amusement in her voice.

"You, too," she said.

Elizabeth latched the door again and led them into the kitchen. "Do you want something to drink?"

Her question seemed to come from a great distance. Juju had been watching her legs, the smooth bulge of her calves, the soft places behind her knees, barely paying attention to what she was saying. She had been looking at girls that way, with an interest in the texture of their flesh, for some time, but she was always afraid that they'd catch her and see into her head, into the places even Juju was a little scared of seeing. So she avoided Elizabeth's eyes, in case Elizabeth saw how much she wanted to put her mouth on the back of her neck. She looked up, down, over at the kitchen tiles, anywhere but directly at this tall and beautiful girl. Later, once they were together, Elizabeth told her it was the most adorable thing she'd ever seen. Juju had expected to collect the guavas and leave, but somehow she was answering yes to the glass of water and then they were talking and it was a few hours before she finally left with the fruit.

The next time they'd met, Elizabeth had come to Juju's house, bringing jam jars for Maja, who insisted that Juju invite her into her room, thinking they would become friends.

Elizabeth kissed Juju for the first time that day, quickly, on her way out.

"You don't need to be so afraid," she'd said. "I like you, too."

And that was it, that was how Juju got a girlfriend.

I think you're great with Elizabeth," Vivek was saying, his long limbs splayed across Juju's bed. "Do you think you're doing a bad job at it?"

Juju rolled over to her side as well, facing him. "I don't tell her everything," she said.

Vivek looked at her, and his eyes were soft and dark pools, floating under long lashes. "We don't tell anyone everything," he said gently. They were lying close enough that Juju could feel his breath drift against her cheekbones. Suddenly the air seemed full of secrets, an iridescent bubble surrounding them.

"What are you not telling me?" she whispered, keeping her voice inside the bubble.

Vivek reached over and stroked a thumb across her cheek. "I tell you everything," he said. "It's other people I don't."

"You don't tell Osita everything?"

His eyes dropped briefly to her mouth. "No," he said, after a pause, dragging his gaze back up to hers. "Not everything."

Heat rushed to Juju's face. She'd thought he'd forgotten—almost thought it was a dream she'd had—what happened the morning after Osita came looking for Vivek at her house. Juju had given the boys their privacy, minding her business, trying not to hear anything that was happening in the room across the corridor. In the morning, she'd woken up early and made some tea, then sat at her bedroom window, looking out at the birds in her mother's garden. When her door creaked open, she already knew it was Vivek. He'd come up to her window seat, dropping a kiss on the top of her head before he sat next to her, tangling his legs with hers. He was shirtless and he smelled like sex. Juju leaned forward and kissed him for the first time, her mug of tea between them, her breath sharp and sweet with mint. She wasn't sure if it surprised him, but Vivek had kissed her back, his morning breath sour on their tongues before he broke it off and nipped his teeth against her nose lightly. "Good morning," he'd said, taking the mug away from her and sipping at it, his hair tousled and dark. He looked out of the window and the morning sun hit his face and Juju wondered why she'd just kissed him. Maybe because he had been hers and now she knew he wasn't, or perhaps he had never been. But Vivek never mentioned the kiss, and even now Juju wasn't sure if he was hinting at it or if she was imagining things.

"What do you keep from Elizabeth?" he asked.

"I don't tell her about you and Osita."

The corner of Vivek's mouth tugged up in amusement. "Why not?"

"It's none of her business, and you know how she is about you." It had taken Elizabeth a long time to forgive Vivek for what happened in the boys' quarters with Osita years ago. Juju had to explain the fugues over and over, explain that Vivek hadn't known what was happening, that he couldn't even remember it. "And you know how she is about Osita. I just—I don't trust her to not be somehow about the two of you being . . ."

"Lovers."

"Yeah."

Vivek watched her face for a moment. "But she's your girlfriend," he said. "Shouldn't you trust her?"

Juju rolled on her back, turning away from him. "Let's talk about something else," she said. She and Elizabeth didn't talk much about their relationship. They were girlfriends, yes, but who could they even go and say that to? And if you didn't tell other people, was it real or was it just something the two of you were telling yourselves? Sometimes Juju found it easier to think of them the way other people did, as close friends. So the question for her became, did she have to tell her close friend about that morning with Vivek? It was just a kiss, it didn't count as anything, so Juju kept quiet.

"Okay," Vivek said. She could feel his gaze on her cheek. "What are you not telling me?"

Juju stared at the ceiling until her vision blurred with tears. "My dad's having an affair."

"What?" He shifted closer to her and put his hand on her braids. "How do you know?"

"They've been fighting and shouting. And I saw him today in the market with his . . . his *other family*, Vivek. With this woman and a little boy." The tears slipped out of her eyes and ran down the sides of her face, spilling into her ears. Vivek wiped some of them away.

"I'm so sorry," he whispered. "Come here."

Juju wrapped her arms around his neck, sobbing into his shoulder. "I feel like a mistake," she said, her voice muffled and thick. "He always wanted a boy. Maybe if I'd been a boy he wouldn't hit Mama so much."

"Shh, don't say that. It's not true."

Juju tried to stop crying, but she couldn't. "He hates us," she sobbed. "He went and replaced us and he won't let Mama go home and her teeth are falling out and he keeps beating her and I can't do anything, Vivek, I can't *do anything.*" Her voice choked on itself, knots of pain clogging up her throat, and Vivek just held her tighter, whispering to her, locking her body against his. Juju wept in his arms for hours, as the afternoon crawled into evening and the light outside dimmed and the sun set and Vivek held her the whole time.

Sixteen

Ebenezer was good at his job.

He'd been a vulcanizer for fifteen years, fixing tires at the same junction the whole time. He was quick with his hands and reliable. Even customers who could have gone to a vulcanizer closer to them would come all the way to Chief Michael Road just to do business with him. All the okada boys in the area preferred him over the other vulcanizers because he never tried to overcharge them; sometimes, if business had been bad for them, he would do repairs on credit. They called him Dede, and when his competitors tried to make trouble for him, the okada boys intervened and there was no more trouble.

Okada drivers were a pack, as anyone who knocked one of them down on the road soon discovered. The boys would surround the car and prevent the driver from escaping, smashing windows and denting doors if they saw fit. Ebenezer liked them, though. They were loud and rough, but they were boys and they reminded him of his junior brothers.

His wife, Chisom, was a trader at the market just down the road, selling fabric and sewing goods. They had been married for six years, but they had no children, which in the past year or two had become a problem. Ebenezer's family blamed Chisom, saying that she was barren or cursed, that something she'd done had blocked her womb. They never liked her because she had managed for herself before she married Ebenezer.

"Be careful of women like that," one of Ebenezer's brothers had told him. "They start feeling like they're men, and before you know it they're trying to run the household themselves, as if you're their houseboy."

Ebenezer had ignored them. He wanted a woman with some business sense, not someone who would be sitting in the house every day waiting for him to provide everything. Besides, she didn't mind the scar on this face, didn't think he was ugly. Someone like Chisom would concentrate on her business, he knew, because that's what she'd always done. Even if—no, when—they had a baby, Ebenezer already knew Chisom would tie it to her back, like the other women at the market, and just continue. He saw himself building a family of hard workers, pulling themselves up in the world, but the absence of a child was obstructing this vision. Everywhere the walls were decked with posters and advertisements about family planning, trying to convince people to slow down on having children, and here they were struggling to have even one. It was humiliating.

Once, after they'd quarreled about it, Chisom had thrown her hands up.

"Every time it's me going to a doctor. Ah-ahn! I don tire. You sef, why don't you go and see if the problem is with you?"

Ebenezer had recoiled in shock. Before he could even reply, she turned over in their bed and pulled her wrapper to cover her, pretending to fall asleep. He sat there for a few minutes, and by the time he thought of something to say, it seemed childish to wake her up, so he went to sleep, too. When he mentioned the conversation to one of his brothers a few days later, his brother laughed.

"Shey I told you?" he said. "Na so she dey blame you because say her womb dey dry. You see wetin you don start?" He went and told the rest of the family, and from there everyone got involved in condemning Chisom and telling Ebenezer what a useless wife he had.

Chisom stopped speaking to her husband because of it, and they started to move around each other like strangers. Ebenezer missed her, but he didn't feel he should apologize for talking to his own family members about his marital problems. Chisom thought that, if he already knew how they felt about her, why would he tell them and give them more ammunition against her? So a silence grew up between them, and Ebenezer was too proud to break it.

He started to look more at other women—not with intent, just a lazy wondering, about what kind of wives they would have been, what it would be like if he'd married one of them and had some children. There was an Abiriba woman who ran a small food stall across the junction from where he worked. Everyone called her Mama Ben and she made the best beans

Ebenezer had ever tasted. She had maybe four or five children, he wasn't sure, and she was still pretty: very clear skin, a nice smile, and she dressed well. Ebenezer wondered what it would be like if he was her husband, with all these children and his wife with a business of her own, just like he always wanted.

He started going to Mama Ben's food stall more and more, sitting at the round plastic table with cardboard folded under one leg to balance it. She always welcomed him with a smile, like she did with every customer, and while it was tempting to believe that the smile she gave him was different, special, Ebenezer knew it wasn't. Still, it was nice to sit there, drink Pepsi, and talk with her other customers. Mama Ben looked at him as if he didn't have that scar on his face, and the only other woman who had done that was Chisom. Ebenezer would stay at the food stall until it was late, keeping an eye out across the road in case a customer stopped by, and then he would wander home filled with goodwill and contentment. He ignored his wife's silence and went to sleep with the memory of Mama Ben's smile in his head.

One evening, when her other customers were gone, he offered to help her out with something in the kitchen, which gave him an excuse to get her alone. There, in a back corner, he plied her with sweet nonsense words and she giggled and he kissed the side of her sweaty neck. She tasted like salt. That night, he reached out in the dark of his bed and tugged at Chisom's hip and she gave in to him, but he wasn't thinking of her, not for any of the time. In fact, it was only with effort that he managed to say her name at one point, and then only because he didn't know Mama Ben's given name, and what else could you call out when you were in bed, really?

Chisom still slept as far away from him on the mattress as she could get, even after they'd had sex. The next morning she didn't speak to him, and this time Ebenezer didn't care. He wasn't even thinking about Mama Ben. No, the woman on his mind now was this orange-seller he'd seen last week, with a sweet voice and a nyash that rolled seductively under her wrapper. She had shown up in his dreams, and he considered this to be a sign. Her hips looked like those of someone who could have children easily. Ebenezer had woken from the dream with an erection, and he thought of the woman as he had a quick breakfast of bread and tea. He looked for her on his way to work, and as he handled his first customer of the day, but he didn't see her. The customer was a banker from Emerald Bank around the corner, sweating in his buttoned shirt and making small talk with a colleague he was giving a lift to, a short woman with fat braids cornrowed onto her head and a sharply ironed polyester skirt.

"I know the manager is afraid I will take his job," the banker was saying. "And why not? The man is lazy! I could be doing the same work that he's doing, if only I was provided the opportunity. You know, that is the key to success." He looked down at his colleague, his face arranged with the seriousness of someone imparting great life advice. "Mark my words. Opportunity is what will land you success in life. When you see the door opening, you must step in! I'm sure your husband has experienced this. Ask him. He will know."

The woman shot him a nasty look but the man completely missed it, his attention diverted by yet another woman, this one walking past Mama Ben's canteen across the street. She was tall with long mammy-water hair in two plaits down her back, wearing a flowered dress that cut off at her calves. Her sandals were plain and brown but her toes had been painted a bright red. She walked like a model and looked like one, thin arms and sharp cheekbones. The banker ogled her, then made kissing noises at her, puckering his lips. When she didn't turn her head, he shouted, "Tall babe! Come make I climb you small!" then burst into uproarious laughter, as if he'd said the wittiest thing. "Is that your hair?" he continued.

"What kind of nonsense question is that?" interrupted his colleague. "Does it look like her hair?"

The banker gave her a contemptuous glance. "Just because your own hair resembles broken broomstick, can somebody not grow their own?"

She ignored the insult. "As long as that? Abeg, it's weave-on. Use common sense."

"It's a lie, I've seen plenty babes with long hair before."

"Biko, all of them are weave-on! Are you stupid?"

"What about those Northern babes, nko? Their own hair grows well."

"Those ones are always plaiting it. Besides, where are you seeing them like that?" She sucked her teeth and rolled her eyes at him.

The banker was thinking hard. "I know I've seen somebody with long long hair like this before. Not this weave-on nonsense you're talking about." He snapped his fingers on alternating hands as if it would call forth the memory. "Somewhere, somewhere."

His colleague took pity on him. "It's okay. After all, it's not as if we can expect you men to even tell the difference when it comes to hair. My brother till today can't tell the difference between extensions and someone's real hair." She laughed at the male ignorance of it all. "He thought that when you relax it, it gets longer and then you can braid it."

"It was at the bank!" her colleague exclaimed, having not listened to anything she'd been saying. "Eh hehn! There were these two girls who came in, and they had this long long fine hair! Kai! I think they were sisters. They were there with their father, but I'm sure their mother was a foreigner."

"Oh," said the woman, sucking her teeth. "If you're talking about half-castes, then that one is different."

"I know those girls," said Ebenezer, tightening the tire he'd just replaced on the man's car. Both bankers looked down at him in surprise, crouched and greasy with worn slippers and dusty feet.

"Ehn, you know them?" The man was smirking as he asked. "How do you know them?"

"Their father is a customer. They look like twins except that one of them is taller, abi?"

The banker nodded grudgingly. "It's true," he said. "That's what I thought also, that maybe they were twins."

The woman was getting impatient with the conversation. "And so? I'm saying that tall woman was wearing weave-on.

End of story." They all turned to look at the woman and her hair again, but she was too far down the road.

The bankers paid Ebenezer and left, and he went back to wondering if the orange-seller would walk by that day or not.

In the weeks that followed, he saw the tall girl a few times. Once she was returning from the market with polythene bags filled with vegetables; another time she was going to the Mr. Biggs at the junction. Once she just seemed to be going for a walk, listening to a Discman in her handbag. Ebenezer decided she must live in the area because she was always walking, never on an okada or in a taxi. She looked like the kind of girl who just liked to walk everywhere. That's probably why she's so slim, he thought.

She usually wore sunglasses, and after that first day her hair was always tied up at the back of her head. Ebenezer could never figure out if it was weave-on or not. He even thought of asking Chisom, but by now she wouldn't even let him touch her at night. "How are we supposed to have a child if you won't even try?" he complained, but she ignored him. Ebenezer knew she wanted him to get checked out at the hospital, but the shame of it was too much, so they just continued like that. Chisom would have known if it was weave-on or not, sha. Her immediate junior sister was a hairdresser.

One afternoon, when there weren't many customers around, he asked Mama Ben instead.

"Ah-ahn. How long have you been watching this girl?" She seemed a little disapproving, so he rushed to reassure her.

"Mba, it was one of the customers who was saying it. Me, I

don't even look at small girls like that. Resembling stockfish. I like proper women." He gestured fullness with his hands and winked at her. She laughed, placated.

"Maybe the girl is from Niger," she suggested. "One of those refugees who are always in the market."

One of Mama Ben's friends chimed in: "Haba now, those ones are beggars. I've seen the girl he's talking about. She looks like she comes from a good family. And besides, she's not fair enough to be one of them. It's probably weave-on. Under it, I'm sure her hair must be like this." She grabbed a tuft of her afro and tugged at it, laughing. Ebenezer laughed as well, his eyes meeting Mama Ben's.

In recent weeks, Mama Ben had told him her name: Florence. He had also found out that she was a widow and had three children, not the four or five he'd previously thought. Her unmarried sister now lived with her, helping to take care of the children. He had even been to her house once, telling Chisom he was doing a house call for a customer in the evening. He hadn't gone inside, had only escorted Mama Ben home and chatted for a bit. She knew her neighbors would talk, but she didn't care. It wasn't as if they knew he was married.

Ebenezer felt he was getting somewhere with her—he wasn't sure where exactly, but he looked forward to it. He was eating rice and stew at her canteen on the day the market burned, savoring the goat meat when the first noises started coming from down the road. As Mama Ben and her customers stood in front of her canteen, peering down the street, sounds filtered toward them slowly, first shouts and then a few alarming screams. Some of the customers hurriedly finished their food and left, heading in the opposite direction from the commotion.

Mama Ben looked worried. "It sounds like one of those riots is starting," she said. "Should I close?"

"Don't you live in that direction?" Ebenezer asked.

"Yes, but I don't want to be in the middle of it. You never know what will happen."

"Wait here," he said. He ran across the road and threw a tarpaulin over his work things, then came back to her. "Pack everything," he said, as he stacked the plastic chairs and took them inside. Mama Ben tilted the tables on their sides and pushed them against the walls. They worked quickly, conscious of the noise growing louder. Ebenezer shoved empty bottles into their crates and dragged them to the back. The last thing he wanted was for convenient glass to be lying around like that. He'd once seen a man struck in the head by a broken bottle, separating scalp neatly from skull before blood filled the gap. It was the worst thing in his memory.

They both pulled down the metal protector, closed the inside doors, and sat there in the cramped space near the shelves of sweets and biscuits. Mama Ben looked scared but calm. There had been so many riots recently that it wasn't much of a surprise to be caught in one.

"I wonder what caused it," she said.

"Maybe the Muslim thing again," he suggested. "You know how people can get about the Northerners."

Mama Ben shook her head. "I don't know why. They're just

people who came here to work, make small money for their families. Why must they always go and disturb them?"

Ebenezer shot her a look. "Because of what's been happening in the North. Are we supposed to just fold our hands and watch how they're treating our brothers and sisters?"

"But it's not the ones here that are doing it. So why disturb them? If you want to disturb anyone, eh hehn—go to the North and look for their trouble there!"

Ebenezer shook his head. He didn't feel like arguing with a woman over this matter.

"Besides," she continued, "it was probably just a thief."

"What makes you think that?"

"Is it not coming from the direction of the market? He probably stole something, and one of the traders shouted, and you know how it goes from there. Tire. Fuel."

Ebenezer sat upright. The market, he thought. The noise was coming from the market. *Chisom was still at the market.*

"Chineke m ee," he said, inhaling air in a short, shocked burst. "My wife is there." He jumped up and started unlocking the door. Mama Ben grabbed his arm.

"They're getting near!" she said. "Don't open the door, abeg."

"And what?" he snapped. "I should leave my wife in the middle of it and hide here with you like a woman?"

"You want to go into the riot? Are you mad? They will just finish you one time."

"Hapu m aka!" He shook off her hand and lifted the protector, ignoring the screeching it made.

Behind him, Mama Ben cursed. "Don't go oo! It's better

you stay here," she warned. "I'm sure your wife is fine. Is it now that she will need you?"

Ebenezer stopped, then turned around and stared at Mama Ben. "What did you say?" She folded her arms stubbornly. He slammed the steel gate down behind him, staring at her in shock through the bars. "You are a wicked woman," he said before he turned away.

"Ebenezer!" she shouted. "Ebenezer!"

He ignored her and stayed on the inside of the crude gutter at the edge of the road as he walked toward the market. In just the few minutes since the first shouts, he could see even from a distance, the scene had deteriorated into chaos. The road was full of cars and okadas with frantic passengers. One man wiped at his head with a handkerchief, stared down at the mess of blood in his hand, then locked eyes with Ebenezer for a moment as the motorcycle whizzed by. Ebenezer swallowed hard and started to jog. He was filled with guilt and shame for having been safely tucked away in Mama Ben's stand without first thinking of his wife, out there at her stall in the market, with no metal protector to hide behind. He wondered if she had run when the chaos started, if she had hopped on an okada, whether he would see her from the side of the road. But he knew Chisom was stubborn, that she wouldn't abandon her merchandise in the market, riot or not. It would be like throwing away money—it would make no sense to her. She probably would have delayed while trying to pack it up, and who knows what could have happened to her in that time? A stray bullet from one of the touts, or the police if they showed up. Jesus Christ, he thought, what if someone got hold of her in the middle of all this madness? What if she were raped? His mind jumped from that and landed on, What if someone raped her and she got pregnant? Nausea swirled through him and he started running. As he got closer to the market, he could see thin dark streams of smoke waving up into the sky. "Chineke, the market is on fire," he whispered to himself, shocked into a halt. Now he was imagining Chisom burned to death, or just burned enough to survive, horribly disfigured, her face peeling off like those women up North who'd been attacked with acid. Ebenezer started running again. He had to save his wife. He couldn't imagine losing her because he'd been with that woman, who had clearly wished evil on Chisom from the beginning. Who knew what she had put in his food? After all, he would normally never behave like that, going to another woman's house. She must have done jazz on him. It had to be. But now he felt as if he'd broken her spell; now it would be okay. As long as he found Chisom.

As he was running, he passed a couple arguing on the side of the road. It was the tall girl with long hair. The man with her was holding her arm, shaking her till her hair fell in her eyes.

"We have to go now!" he was shouting. "Do you know what they'll do to you?"

She pulled away from him so hard that she stumbled backward. Ebenezer saw her skirt flutter in the air, covered in small red flowers, but then he was past them and they were behind him and he couldn't hear anything over the noise in his head and the air.

When he got closer to the mob, he slowed to a quick walk, trying to keep to the side. People bumped his shoulders and he was pushed a few times, but no one really disturbed him. They were focused on wherever they were going. Later he learned that most of them were heading to the area near the mosque, in the main market on Chief Michael Road, where a group of Hausa people plied their trade as shoemakers in a little market. An altercation there between a Hausa trader and an Igbo customer, a prominent shop owner, had escalated until the Hausa trader slapped the shop owner. In moments a crowd had gathered, coiled and furious, ready to make every other Northerner pay for that one man and his impertinence. This was not their town—they couldn't talk anyhow here and expect to get away with it.

Ebenezer waded through whole sections of the market, now in ruins, the air full of smoke from the parts that were still burning. The muddy alleys were strewn with bolts of colorful fabric trampled by many feet; vendors scrambled about, trying to salvage them from the muck, crying and swearing and afraid. The smoke was worse by the time he got to Chisom's shop, where she sold buttons and needles and sewing machine parts and thread. This area was already deserted. Some of the stores had been locked in haste, as if that could protect them from fire. Others had goods tossed about in front of them, discarded by traders who had tried to carry their merchandise away but found their arms overfull. He reached the wooden door to Chisom's shop, with its flaking light blue paint, and coughed as he called her name. Particles of soot had settled on the white fabric draped for sale in the doorway.

"Chisom!" he shouted.

"Ebenezer?" She emerged from the back, her face marked with dried tears, but calm. "You came!"

He rushed forward and embraced his wife, who stood numb and shocked in the circle of his arms. "You came all this way," she said, disbelieving.

"Are you all right?" he asked, patting her face.

Chisom nodded. "I was packing up the things as fast as I could."

"Forget the things, jo! Can't you smell the smoke? You want to stay here and wait for the fire to reach you?"

"I've almost finished. I just didn't know how to carry them out. We can't afford to lose the merchandise."

Ebenezer looked at his wife and the determination hammered into her face. Her tenacity, he realized, was something he could learn from. How to stand in the face of actual fire and not run, how to do what it took for them to survive because she'd decided to. She could have been hurt, could have been killed, but she had done it anyway. Ebenezer felt ashamed at how hard he'd been fighting her about seeing a doctor. She had packed up the things, not knowing how she could carry all of it, simply because she was ready to handle that part when the time came. Now the time had come and he was there, as he should have been, as he always should have been. Why should she be carrying anything by herself when he was her husband?

"I'm here now," Ebenezer said. Chisom gave him a small, unsure smile and he embraced her one more time. "Let's go," he said. He carried most of the Ghana-must-go bags she'd packed and they made their way out of the market, stumbling slightly but together. They flagged down an okada who recognized Ebenezer, and together they climbed aboard, balancing the bags awkwardly as they left the market behind.

Most of the market burned to the ground that day. It was years before the government got around to rebuilding it.

Seventeen

Vivek

Here is one of my favorite memories with Osita. We are in my bedroom. My parents are out and we are alone. I am lying with my head on his bare stomach and he's playing with my hair, pulling on the curls and watching them spring back. Sometimes he rubs my scalp and I turn my head to kiss his ribs.

"I had a dream," I tell him.

He looks down from the pillows surrounding him. "Tell me," he says, in that way where I know he's genuinely interested, he wants to hear my dreams, my stories.

"I dreamt that I was our grandmother," I tell him. "I looked in a mirror and she was there, just like the pictures, and she spoke to me in Igbo."

"What did she say?"

"*Hold my life for me.*" I wait for his laugh, but it never comes. "Do you believe in reincarnation?" I ask him.

"I'm not sure my belief matters," he says. "If it is, it is, whether I believe it or not."

"You know what I'm asking."

My cousin gives me a small smile and twists some of my hair in his fingers. "They talk about you and her in the village, did you know?"

I have never heard this before. I sit halfway up, leaning against his body.

"They talk about how she died the same day you were born," he continues, "how my father got into an argument with your dad about your name. But you weren't a girl, so . . ." Osita shrugs, lets the story die off.

"What do you think?" I ask him.

My cousin looks at me with a gentleness he shows to no one else. "Who are we to define what is impossible or not?"

"You're just saying that," I tell him.

He shakes his head. "I mean it. You know what's been happening in your head. You're the only person who knows. So ask yourself if it feels right, and somewhere, deep inside of you, there's a compass that will tell you whether you're right or wrong."

I smile at him. "Is this how you make decisions?" I tease.

His eyes sweep over both of us, naked on the bed, and he doesn't smile back. I feel a thrill as his gaze touches me; I know it is a precursor to his hands, his mouth, the marvelous rest of him.

"Only the important ones," he replies, and then he reaches for me.

Eighteen

Three months after Vivek died, Chika tried to force Kavita to stop asking people about him. She didn't listen to him, of course. She thought it was a ridiculous thing to ask—as if she could stop, as if there was any reason on this earth why she should stop. Her son was dead and buried in the village, in Ahunna's compound, next to her grave. Chika had put a concrete slab over the ground where Vivek's body was; Kavita tried not to imagine it crushing him. She would have spent all her time beside it, but the answers weren't there. They had carved an inscription into the concrete. VIVEK OJI, it said. BELOVED SON.

Chika had wanted to add more, but he didn't know what else to say and Kavita had other things on her mind, like finding out what had happened to him, so the two of them left it like that. Besides, it said everything—he was beloved, by his parents and his friends—and that, Kavita supposed, was why none of those friends were talking to her, even though all she wanted to know was what had happened to her son.

Just that morning, Vivek had had breakfast with them. He had stayed at home the night before, instead of running off to Maja's or Rhatha's or Ruby's house. Kavita was delighted. In the morning, Vivek had tied his hair in a bun on top of his head, twisting it up tightly, then taken a bath and brushed his teeth. Kavita had watched him spoon heaps of powdered milk over a bowl of cornflakes, then tilt a thermos of hot water over the bowl and stir it around, and she had smiled. This had been his favorite breakfast since he was small. Of course he picked out his three cubes of sugar, let them dissolve into the milk; of course he ate the cornflakes quickly—he'd never liked them soggy—then tipped the bowl to his mouth and drank the sweetened milk. Kavita remembered every second of it as if she was back at the table with him: the last time she would ever watch her child feed himself. That act of putting nourishment into his body—it was such an alive thing to do.

In that same day, only hours away from the breakfast table, Vivek would be lying on the veranda, his body cooling in her arms. How can? It wasn't possible.

He'd told her that morning that he was going to see the girls. She didn't know which house he meant; by then, the girls had blended into an amorphous group, Juju and Elizabeth or Somto and Olunne or any other combination. Their houses were the only places he visited. Even before the burial, Kavita had asked them all if they'd seen him, if they knew anything about what happened.

"He came to our house first," Somto told her. The girls lived with their parents in a white duplex in a residential area near the glass factory. "We were making pancakes for breakfast."

"But he'd already had breakfast," Kavita said, her eyes swollen from weeping. She was twisting one of Chika's handkerchiefs in her fingers, the damp cotton taut against her skin. Somto smiled a little. She'd been crying, too. "It was pancake day, Aunty Kavita. He always comes for pancake day."

Kavita frowned. "I didn't know that. Since when?"

The girl shrugged. She had braided cornrows that crawled into two large plaits dropping down her back. "Since he came back from uni. We invited him that day when we came to your house for the first time. His favorite part was flipping the pancakes. When we first tried to teach him how to do it, everything just splattered on the floor. It was such a mess!" She gave a small laugh that quickly trailed away. "But then he got really good at it. I can't . . . I can't believe he's gone."

The girl broke into tears and all Kavita could feel was drained. It was interesting, she thought, how people mourned Vivek. Somehow she felt like they didn't have the right to cry in front of her. After all, was it their son who had died? Was it them that had held that baby on the day he was born? No, it was just the two of them together in the hospital as Ahunna died, just Kavita and her child in that bed, all mixed up in love and uncertainty, Chika beside them like an afterthought. She regretted what had happened next—the depression that followed, when she pulled away from her child in grief. She should have held him tighter, as the world was whirling around them. It had always been her and her baby.

The loss of him felt cumulative, as if he'd been slipping away so slowly that she'd missed the rift as it formed in his childhood. It was only once he'd become a man that she realized she couldn't reach him anymore, that he was gone, so gone that breath had left his body. No one else could feel that lifetime of loss. No one else had lost him more than she had, yet they cried in front of her as if it meant something. They're still children, Kavita tried to tell herself, not mature enough to do her the courtesy of keeping their tears in their bedrooms, among their own complete families. But still she thought of them as selfish brats without home training or compassion or empathy, and this in turn made her angry at these girls she knew she still loved, somewhere under the rage and pain and the grief that she felt belonged to her and only her.

She even had trouble sharing it with her husband, but it was easier with him because he'd fallen into that same darkness that had taken him when his mother died. Chika's grief dragged down every centimeter of his skin, pulling muscles and bones along with it, making it hard for him to stand up. He took time off work, lying in bed in a singlet that grew dirtier every day. Once in a while, when she issued a tired command, he'd drag himself out of bed, wash himself with blank eyes, and climb into bed again. Kavita didn't feel inclined to try any harder to get him out of it. She knew about him and Eloise—he wasn't intelligent enough to hide it from her, and he'd been faithful up till then. It was so obvious when he stopped; all the little changes were stark and loud. She didn't mind what his grief was turning him into. Part of her felt like he deserved to go mad: while she had been pouring herself into their child, he had been pouring himself into her friend.

She hoped he never found his way out of that bed. She hoped he would rot inside it.

Eloise even had the nerve to be calling and checking on them. Kavita started hanging up the phone whenever she heard her voice. Let the woman figure out what she knew. She wouldn't have picked up the phone at all, except for the chance that it could be one of the girls calling with information about Vivek, something they hadn't confessed to her yet. She also hung up when Mary or Ekene called. To Kavita, they were now the same person, and she would never forgive them for what had happened at their church. Chika had insisted on inviting them to the burial, but once that was over, as far as Kavita was concerned, so were they.

While Chika lay in their bed, Kavita stayed in Vivek's room. She ran her hands over the walls, over the posters he'd ripped out of pop magazines Eloise had brought back from the UK. The woman's interest in her child seemed false and ugly now; perhaps it had all been a way to get close to Chika. Kavita reminded herself that it didn't matter. Eloise could have Chika if she wanted. Nothing mattered. Her eyes ran over the pictures without really registering them: Missy Elliott. Puff Daddy.

En Vogue. Backstreet Boys. He had put them all up before he went off to uni. Kavita wondered why he hadn't taken them down afterward, once he'd changed. Or maybe he hadn't changed as much as it seemed. At night, now, she slept in his bed and cried. Sometimes she thought she could hear Chika crying, too, through the wall, but she never went to him.

Sitting across from Somto in Rhatha's sitting room, Kavita watched the girl cry and thought how ridiculous it was that she could still look so pretty even while sobbing. There were no inelegant strings of mucus swinging from her nose, no shiny saliva pooling in her mouth when she opened it to wail. Somto wept mostly with tears, gleaming against her skin as they fell. She dabbed at them with the hem of her dress, the skirt full and wide, leaving enough material to cover her thighs even as she bent to reach her face.

"I'm sorry, Aunty Kavita," she said. "I know this must be terrible for you."

Terrible, Kavita thought. What a word. Did it feel like terror? More like horror, actually. Terrible sounded like it had a bit of acceptance in it, like an unthinkable thing had happened but you'd found space in your brain to acknowledge it, perhaps even begin to accept it. Then again, horrible sounded the same way. The words had departed from their origins. They were diluted, denatured. She looked up and realized that Somto was looking at her, sitting there in silence.

"I just want to know how this happened," Kavita said. "What time did he leave here?"

Somto thought for a bit. "Maybe around twelve o'clock? He didn't say where he was going. We all assumed he was going to see Juju."

"Are you sure he didn't say? What of Olunne? Maybe she'll remember what he said."

Somto looked at Kavita, a bit concerned. "Aunty, you can just ask Juju. I know she saw him that day, but I don't know if he went straight from here."

"Where is your sister? I want to ask her also."

"She's not here. She went out with our mum." Somto stood up. Kavita could see the discomfort wafting off her. "But I'm sure Juju is at home with Aunty Maja. You can go and ask her." Somto must have known she was being rude, but she didn't seem to care. "I have to go and run some errands," she added. "My mum will be angry if I don't finish them before she gets home."

Kavita stood up, already thinking of what she could ask Juju and Maja. "Tell your mother and sister I'll come back another time to ask them," she told Somto, who made a mental note to avoid Kavita for a while. She would tell her mother about Kavita's questions, and perhaps Rhatha wouldn't force her or Olunne to sit through this kind of questioning, as if it was their fault that something had happened to their friend.

"Yes, Aunty," she said, though. "I'll tell them."

"Don't forget."

"I won't."

Kavita picked up her bag and started to leave. "It's important."

"I know, Aunty." Somto closed the door and leaned against it, exhaling in relief.

Kavita stood outside and looked around the yard, trying to imagine how Vivek would have seen it on that his last day, when he was leaving: the sky wide above him, the orange tree spilling over the fence. He might have stood in front of this door, looked up at the clouds and seen shapes in them, as he had when he was a child. Kavita folded her arms around herself and walked to where she'd parked the car. She drove to Maja's house in a partial daze, slow enough that cars around her kept blasting their horns. A few of the drivers leaned out of their windows to insult her. She didn't hear any of it.

Maja greeted her at their front door with a tight hug. Kavita tried to return it, but her arms were tired and limp. She let Maja lead her into the sitting room and pour her some tea. "Drink it," Maja said, and Kavita held the cup in both hands, feeling the warmth seep into her palms.

"I just came from Rhatha's house," she said.

"You should be resting, my dear."

"Her daughter said Vivek was there on the day he died. And then he came here."

Maja gazed at her friend sadly. "What are you doing, Kavita? You can't keep going over this. It's not good for you."

"Did he come here?"

Maja sighed. "I was at work all day that day. He might have.

He usually did." She put a hand on Kavita's knee. "Why are you asking all this?"

"I have to know what happened. My son can't just die like that."

"It was an accident, no? That's what Chika told Charles. It was a car accident? And someone brought him to the house?"

Kavita looked up at her friend slowly, a frown tightening her forehead. "An accident," she said.

"Someone recognized him, didn't they?"

"They must have . . ." Kavita hadn't known this was the story Chika was telling people. "How else would they know whose house to bring him to? It had to be someone who actually knew him."

"Well, who brought him to the house?" asked Maja. She didn't use the word "body," and Kavita noted the small kindness.

"Nobody," she said.

Maja looked confused. "Nobody brought him to the house?"

"No." Kavita shook her head. "I don't— We don't know who brought him to the house."

There was a pause before Maja spoke again, carefully. "You mean you didn't see the person? You didn't talk to them?"

Kavita's eyes filled with tears.

"No. We didn't see anybody. They just . . . they just left him. They just left him in front of the door like he was rubbish." Kavita broke down into sobs and Maja came beside her and hugged her.

"My dear, that's terrible," she said. "I'm so sorry."

"I just need to find out what happened to him. The police

are useless and Chika just looks at me when I try to talk to him
about it. He asks what difference will it make."

"I understand why you need to. It has to make sense."

Kavita nodded. "He was so young. Something happened. It
doesn't make sense. They took off his clothes when they left
him there."

Maja recoiled. "What?! Who would do something like that?"

"I don't know. I don't know anything. That's what I have to
find out. That's why I need to talk to Juju. I need to know what
happened when he came to visit, what time he left, things like
that. I just need to find out, Maja. I can't sleep until I do."

Maja's face closed up a little. "I'm sorry, Kavita. . . . You can't
talk to Juju right now."

Kavita looked confused. "Why not? Isn't she around?"

"Well, yes, she's in her room. But Kavita, she hasn't said
anything since she found out."

"Anything about that day, you mean?"

"No, I mean she hasn't said anything at all. She's . . . stopped
talking. That's why Charles came back."

Kavita blinked. She hadn't even realized that Charles was
back, although she'd noticed him at the burial. But she hadn't
asked Maja why he came, because she didn't care. What did a
broken marriage matter in the face of a dead child? This was
how Kavita knew she was a terrible person—that she could
know the things Charles had put Maja through, see the strain
in Maja's face, and not care. But terrible people could still be
good mothers. The last thing she could do for Vivek was to find
out what had happened. Maja was still talking. "We're just

trying to be there for her right now. Obviously she and Vivek were very close and she's taking this really hard. We have to be patient with her." She sounded as if she was trying to convince herself. "At least Charles is no longer talking about moving that woman into my house." Maja spat out "that woman" as if it tasted bad, but relief ran under her words. Kavita knew she was supposed to express some sympathy, but she remained silent.

Maja caught her lack of response and smoothed out her face. "She won't talk to you, Kavita. And I don't even think it's a good idea to ask her about him. It's just too painful for her."

Kavita stared. She couldn't have heard right. "Did you—did you just say it's too painful for her?"

"Yes, of course. You know how much they loved each other."

A cracked laugh burst out from Kavita's mouth. She couldn't help it. "I'm his mother!" she gasped, incredulous. "It's too painful for *her*? Do you know how ridiculous that sounds?"

For a moment, Maja didn't respond. "Kavita," she said eventually, her voice level, "of course you're his mother. That doesn't mean there aren't other people who loved him, who are mourning him as well."

"I don't care!" Kavita stood up quickly, her heart racing. "If you people really loved him, you would be helping me find out what happened to him! But instead all you want to do is block me from finding out the truth. What kind of love is that?"

Maja stood up as well. "My dear, of course I want to help you find out what happened. We all do. All I'm saying is that Juju can't help you right now. She's suffering—"

"I don't care about her suffering!" Kavita hissed, and Maja recoiled. "It is *nothing* compared to my own. That girl will answer my questions and then she can go and suffer in peace!" She took a step forward, but Maja stepped in front of her with a hard, set face.

"I said no, Kavita. Absolutely not." They glared at each other. "I know you're going through unimaginable pain right now," Maja said, "but it is my job to protect my child and I can't let you speak with her. Not when you're like this."

Kavita felt as if Maja had hit her. "Are you saying I didn't protect my child?" she whispered, her voice splintering.

Maja's face softened.

"Oh, Kavita, of course I'm not saying that."

"It sounds like you are! So my child is dead because I didn't protect him, ehn?"

Maja sighed, her eyes sympathetic. "Go home, Kavita. Go home, rest and grieve. You're not thinking correctly." She tried to put a hand on her friend's arm, but Kavita wrenched it away. She snatched up her handbag, then pushed past Maja and out the door, slamming it behind her.

Inside her bedroom, Juju sat curled up by the door, her ear pressed to the wood as she listened to their quarrel. She was wearing a cotton nightgown that she hadn't changed in a day or two. Juju nervously pumped her mouth full of saliva then swallowed, words knocking about in her head. She was a little surprised to hear her mother defend her so vehemently; she'd even wondered if she would use Vivek's grieving mother as a tool to break her silence. But to be left protected, inside the bubble of silence she had created when she found out he was dead—that was a mercy Juju welcomed. She didn't know why she'd stopped talking, to be honest. It had just felt easier. People had kept asking her how she was, how she was holding up, if she was okay, but when they realized she wasn't going to answer, they eventually stopped.

Vivek's death had even managed to bring her father home and it felt a little bit like they were a family again. If the other woman was still a factor, she was sure she would have heard her parents arguing about it by now. Somto and Olunne had stopped by, but Juju simply left the sitting room when they came, and locked herself in her bedroom. It was harder to be silent around them; she had to run away to keep the bubble intact, so she could be safe inside it. Elizabeth hadn't come by the house, but she had called several times, and Maja could only respond that Juju wasn't speaking yet. Elizabeth had even sent her a letter. Juju read it sitting on her bedroom floor, leaning against the bed frame:

> *Dear Juju,*
>
> *I don't know what to say about all of this. Your mumsy says that you're still not talking to anybody and after what happened last time we spoke in person, you probably don't want to talk to me either. I tried to greet you at the burial and you just ignored me. I can't lie and say that I'm not still angry with you, but it's somehow for me to continue*

*to be angry in this situation. I want to help you but
I'm angry with you but Vivek is dead.*

*Everything is just a mess. I don't even know
why I'm writing this. Maybe you can write back if
you still don't want to talk? I can't keep calling your
house like this just to make sure you're okay. If I'm
being honest, I'm still angry with him, too. How
can I be angry at someone who's dead? And not just
dead, but they killed him. I feel like a horrible
person. It should have been enough to forgive both
of you, that whole thing people like to say about
realizing life is short and cherishing your loved ones,
but it doesn't feel that way to me. I never even got to
talk to him about it.*

*I don't know where I'm going with this. I just
know I'm still angry.*

Sorry.

xx
Elizabeth

Juju folded the letter and put it inside one of her books. She
hadn't seen Elizabeth since about a week before Vivek was
killed, when she'd told her the truth about the morning after
Osita came to her house looking for his cousin. She had been
tired of hiding it from Elizabeth. Every time her girlfriend
whispered *I love you*, Juju had wanted to say it back, but that
morning was blocking her throat and the words wouldn't come

out. She knew Elizabeth was hurt and confused by her silence; she'd said so more than once.

"I know you love me," she'd said. "Why won't you say it out loud? Are you afraid it will make this too real, or what? Are you ashamed of us?"

It frustrated Juju as well. She knew she loved Elizabeth and she wanted to tell everyone, even their parents. The possessiveness she'd felt over Vivek had faded, and in its wake she could recognize what real love was, that it was what shimmered in the air between her and Elizabeth. Juju wanted to hold her hand anywhere—in front of their friends and family, when they were all at each other's houses. She wanted to be able to cuddle on the sofa and not have people think there was something abnormal about it. It wasn't fair—there were times when people assumed she and Vivek were together, and no one seemed to have a problem with that. If anything, it made Vivek seem a little more "normal," it made people more comfortable with him. But she and Elizabeth were a different story.

And then Elizabeth was there, thinking that Juju agreed with these people on some level—that they had something to be ashamed of. It wasn't true, but Juju didn't know how to tell Elizabeth about what really worried her: What if she left? What would she do if she lost Elizabeth? Juju loved her more than she'd loved any boy, and Elizabeth said she felt the same way. She told Juju about Osita, and then about a senior girl at her school who'd introduced her to options that went beyond useless boys. The senior girl had taught her things, things she then taught Juju—like how being with a girl was so much better than being with a boy, because boys were selfish and they didn't know how to make you feel good. Girls knew how to touch each other properly.

Still, both Juju and Elizabeth were scared that one of them would wake up someday and decide she was tired of being with a girl. This was why Juju didn't want to tell Elizabeth about the kiss with Vivek. She'd always sworn he was just her best friend, there was nothing going on, she was sure Vivek liked boys. Elizabeth had believed her. Why shouldn't she? It wasn't like she knew she was dating a liar—not yet.

When Juju finally told her about the kiss, Elizabeth looked stunned. Juju watched as shock and pain cycled through her face, quickly replaced by disbelief. "Wait, is this not the same Vivek you kept telling me there was nothing going on with?" Elizabeth asked, then laughed in an empty way. "Wow, I've really been an idiot. You've been here making a fool of me this whole time. I hail you!"

"It's not like that," Juju tried to say. "Let me explain—"

"It's not like what? You missed penis so much that you had to make a move on Vivek, of all people? He's not even a man, for God's sake."

"Elizabeth!"

"I don't even blame him. We all know his head is somewhere else. But you—how long have you been lying to me about this? What else have you two done?" Elizabeth held up a hand and looked at Juju with disgust. "In fact, don't tell me. I can't even tolerate your face right now."

She walked away and Juju ran after her, trying to grab her

arm, but Elizabeth shook her off. Juju called her name, her voice breaking, not caring who heard or saw, but Elizabeth never looked back.

A week later, Maja came into Juju's room to tell her that Vivek was gone, that he had "passed away"—useless words meant to make death feel better. Juju stared back at her as the news of his death ground to powder the pieces Elizabeth had left her heart in, until there was nothing remaining in her chest to come up through her throat. That was why she stopped talking, and Kavita's visit didn't change that. Nothing changed that until one morning when Juju dreamt of Vivek and he kissed her again in the dream, and a river flowed from his tongue down her throat. Juju woke up with a dry mouth, but when Maja said good morning, Juju said it back to her automatically and watched the joy flood her mother's face. Charles was there—he was always there now—and when Juju greeted him, she was surprised to see her father look both old and relieved.

The next time Kavita came to visit, her face thin and tired, Juju told her what she wanted to know: that Vivek had come to her house that day, but he'd left in the afternoon and she thought he'd gone home. She told Kavita he'd eaten lunch there, but he hadn't had much because he was full of pancakes.

"So you don't know what happened to him?" Kavita asked, her eyes full of disappointment.

"I'm so sorry, Aunty. I really don't. I thought he got home safe. I didn't know what happened until—" Juju's voice cracked and she paused to force it back into one piece. "Until you called my mother."

"They put him in front of the door, you know." Kavita looked so frail.

"I know, Aunty. I heard." Maja was waiting just outside the parlor and Juju threw her a look, begging for rescue.

Her mother swooped in and put her hands on Kavita's shoulders. "Come now," she said. "Let's get you some tea. Juju, you can go to your room."

Juju leaned down to give Kavita a quick hug before she left, feeling how sharp her shoulder blades were, like a wishbone ready to snap. Juju wanted to whisper that she loved her, but it wasn't the kind of thing any of them ever said out loud and she knew it wouldn't make a difference. Still, seeing Kavita like that, almost going mad with trying to figure out what had happened to Vivek, she wondered if Vivek's mother deserved a bit more of the truth—if she and the others were hurting her every time she asked them the wrong questions and they gave her their careful answers. The truth was so far away from any of her suspicions that she had no chance of interrogating them successfully; she didn't know how much she didn't know. She was Vivek's mother, and she was wasting away before their eyes. They were as guilty as she suspected. They were making her suffer.

Juju called Elizabeth.

"I didn't think I was going to hear from you again," Elizabeth said when she picked up.

Juju ignored her. "We have to tell Aunty Kavita the truth," she said. "It's time."

Nineteen

Osita

Juju called to say we were meeting at the sports club on Sunday. She and Elizabeth were already there when I arrived, sitting far enough apart to tell me they were still quarreling, even though their bodies were unconsciously angled toward each other. Juju was tapping her foot against the grass, her legs crossed. Elizabeth was barely moving. I could feel the anger layered quietly inside her as she sat in the plastic chair, staring into emptiness.

Ever since that day in the boys' quarters, Elizabeth and I had tried not to be around each other too much. When she and Juju got involved, it got harder to avoid each other, since we were all connected by Vivek—who she forgave a lot faster than she forgave me, by the way. But no wahala. I stayed in Owerri and minded my business and everything was cool. Besides, the Elizabeth I'd been with was very different from who she was now, with her shaved head and thick eyeliner. Other girls would have worn big earrings and lipstick to compensate for cutting their hair, as if they were still in secondary school, but Elizabeth clearly didn't care. Sometimes I wanted to tell her she looked like such a lesbian that it was a miracle Aunty Maja hadn't realized she was knacking her daughter—but, again, I was minding my business.

Juju stood up and hugged me when I got to their table. She held me for a little too long and I saw Elizabeth's eyes narrow. "Thank you for coming all that way," she whispered. I had stayed in Owerri after Aunty Kavita collected me from Port Harcourt. I couldn't go back to Vivek's house, but the grief had stretched to mine anyway. My mother cried a lot, though I never knew if it was because he'd died or because she'd let him slip out of her hands. I never asked. My father walked around, age drawing down the skin of his face, barely even talking to my mother. I knew he wanted to be there for Uncle Chika and it was killing him that their wives had dug this gaping gutter between them.

"We are brothers," he had said once, when I asked how he was, wonder and disbelief in his voice. "We are still brothers, yet he won't talk to me." I almost said I knew how it felt to lose a brother, but it was too complicated a feeling to put into words, so I kept it inside my chest.

"You said it was important," I reminded Juju as we broke our embrace.

Juju sniffed and wiped her nose. "It is. We're just waiting for the others."

"Elizabeth," I said in greeting, nodding at her.

"Osita." She flicked her eyes at me and smiled tightly with her lips closed, her tone spiked. "Glad you could make it."

By then, I figured Juju must have told her about my relationship with Vivek. I wasn't surprised by her hostility, and I didn't care enough to make noise about it. What was there to fight about? The boy was dead. I sat down and waited, glancing over at Juju. She looked exhausted. She'd taken her light brown hair out of its usual braids and tied it into a rough bun; she had bags under her eyes, no lip gloss, and yet she was the most beautiful I could remember seeing her, even looking like she was about to break. It was strange—the next thought I had was, Vivek would want me to take care of her. "How have you been?" I asked.

"She's fine," Elizabeth snapped. I almost snapped back at her, but then Somto and Olunne arrived and we were all greeting one another, rearranging chairs, passing around menus. Juju and Elizabeth had to move their chairs closer to make room for Somto and Olunne, overriding the little force field between them, and in that absence they fell back into their old comfort, their voices lacing together like one fabric. We put in our order with the waiter, then Olunne turned to Juju. "Okay," she said. "What's this about? Why did we bring Osita all the way from Owerri?"

Juju and Elizabeth looked at each other and Elizabeth gave her a small nod. "Show them," she said.

Juju reached inside her bag and pulled out a colorful envelope, bright stock-photo faces smiling all over it. "I got this developed the other day from Vivek's camera," she said, handing the envelope to Somto, who was sitting next to her. "I—I think we should give them to Aunty Kavita."

Somto opened the envelope and inhaled a soft, quick breath. She looked at Juju, upset.

"You took pictures of him like this?"

Juju's jaw tightened. "He wanted them. Was I supposed to tell him no?"

Somto closed the flap of the envelope without looking at the other photographs inside it. "So you mean the people at the photo place also saw these?"

Elizabeth rolled her eyes. "Use your brain," she said. "Of course they did. And so what?" Olunne reached across the table and took the envelope from her sister. "You've already seen them, Elizabeth?"

"I went with Juju to pick them up."

Somto looked furious. "You shouldn't have taken these pictures, Juju. I don't care if that's what he wanted. What if someone finds them? What if someone at the photo place made their own copies?"

"Didn't you hear her?" Olunne was sifting through the pictures; her voice was gentle, almost amused. "She wants to show them to his mother."

"You dey craze," Somto said to Juju. "Do you hear me? Your head is not correct. Aunty Kavita must never see these. Can you imagine what it will do to her?"

"I think she should know." Juju sounded uncertain, afraid.

Elizabeth put a hand on her arm. "You knew him best," she said.

"He's not here!" shouted Somto. Elizabeth glared at her and she lowered her voice. "He's not here," she repeated. "They buried him already. What's the point of showing her these?"

Olunne handed me the photographs and I took them, my heart beating fast. I already knew what I would see, that it would hit me in the chest like a lorry. I hadn't seen a picture of him since the burial.

"You don't see what she's like," Juju argued. "She's been asking questions all the time. She won't stop. She wants to know what happened to him."

"We don't know what happened to him," said Olunne.

"Well, she thinks we do. Or at least that I do, just because he was at my house last."

"She was coming to our house, but she's stopped," Somto said.

"Yes, because it's me that she's disturbing!" Juju retorted. "Do you know she and my mother quarreled about it? Mumsy even said she shouldn't come to the house anymore—after all these years they've been friends. So now she just calls our landline all the time, begging me to remember something that I'm not telling her."

"And it's this you want to tell her?" Somto's eyebrows were raised and mocking. "You don't think these will cause more questions?"

Juju shrugged. "They're the truth. She knows he was hiding something. Why don't we just show her?"

"Because the woman is nearly mad, Juju." Olunne said it

like she was stating a gentle fact. I kept looking through the photographs, the gloss slipping off my fingers. There I was in one of them, smiling for the camera. I remembered that one. Juju had taken it in the late afternoon when the sun was setting and had become a line across her bedroom wall. Light cut through my face severely, casting my smile in shadows. I put the photo at the bottom of the pile and continued looking through the rest as the girls argued.

"Elizabeth, please come and collect your girlfriend," Somto said, throwing her hands up. "She won't stop talking nonsense."

"No, but seriously." Olunne turned to Elizabeth. "Do you think we should tell Aunty Kavita?"

Elizabeth bit her lip. "Look," she said, "eventually all secrets come out. It's just a matter of time. And the longer it takes, the worse it is in the end." She lifted and dropped one shoulder. "We all know this from experience, abi?"

I almost felt Juju wince and knew she was thinking of her father. Or maybe the secrets she'd kept from Elizabeth.

Somto wasn't convinced. "How will she find out?" she asked. "Na you go tell am? In fact, apart from all of us here, who even knew about it?" No one said anything. "Exactly. So unless one of us decides to go and start opening their big mouth, there's no reason Aunty Kavita should know. You people don't have any respect. Let the woman remember Vivek the way she knew him, haba! What's your own? Am I the only one with sense here?"

Olunne folded her hands and nodded. "Why cause trouble?" she said.

Juju and Elizabeth looked at each other. "Two against two," Elizabeth said, and they all turned to me.

"I think Osita should decide," said Juju.

Somto sucked her teeth. "Why him?"

My heart sped up. Was Juju about to tell them about us?

Olunne smacked her sister's arm. "Idiot. Vivek is his cousin. It's his family we're talking about."

Juju nodded. "She's your aunt. You decide."

Elizabeth's mouth curled into a snarl. "Yes," she said, her voice saccharine. "He was your cousin." She was looking me straight in the eye; I could see her disgust. I wondered how much Juju had told her, or if it even mattered at this point.

Juju glared briefly at Elizabeth, then turned to me again. "Should she know?"

I opened my mouth to answer, but then our food came and I swallowed the words. We all fell silent for a bit, shifting things around to make space on the table.

After the waiter left, Juju took a piece of fried yam and waited for my answer. Elizabeth started eating her suya, her eyes on my face. The sisters blew on the bowl of pepper soup they were sharing, and I stared down at my plate for a moment, looking at the oil-slick ugba and the blackness of the fried snail. The smell was rich and thick in my nostrils.

"Show her," I said, surprising even myself.

"Jesus Christ," said Somto.

Juju coughed on a piece of yam. "Wait, really?" She hadn't expected me to agree. She thought I'd want to hide him.

"Show them to her," I repeated, closing the envelope and handing it back to Juju.

"You people are going to kill that woman," said Somto. "Wallahi."

I ignored that. "You're right," I said to Juju. "She needs answers. We're all pretending he wasn't killed. As if Vivek dying was a normal thing."

"But we know *why* he was killed," muttered Olunne, poking her straw into her glass.

"Exactly," I said. "We know. But she doesn't. So show her, so that she can understand. So she can stop asking questions."

"If you think that's going to stop her from asking questions, you're mad." Somto picked up her spoon and swirled it in the pepper soup.

"No, she'll continue asking questions. But she'll ask different ones. And maybe they'll be questions we can answer."

Juju looked like she was about to cry. "Thank you," she said. "I just can't be lying like this."

"Jesus," said Olunne. "This is going to be crazy. If you tell her, all our parents are going to know. That means they're going to ask us questions. All of us. Why we allowed it. Why we didn't tell them."

"It wasn't their business," said Juju.

"Is that so? I want to be there when you tell that to your mother. I'm sure she'll understand." Olunne dumped her straw in the glass and folded her arms. "This is going to be a disaster. They're going to kill us."

"At least we're alive," Juju said. "Vivek isn't."

The table fell silent. Then Somto put her face in her hands and groaned. "I can't believe you're going to make us do this."

I stared at my food, my appetite gone, my chest tightening from seeing his pictures. "I have to start getting back to Owerri," I said, standing up. The girls looked up at me, surprised.

"You're not staying with Aunty Kavita?" Somto asked.

I shook my head. "I told my mother I'd come back tonight."

"You should stay," Olunne said. "It's not safe to travel all the way to Owerri this late."

"It's fine. I've done it before."

Juju stood up. "I'll walk you out," she offered. I said goodbye and watched Elizabeth watch her as we left the table. We walked through the front building and the lobby, stopping just outside the gate.

"Are you sure you have to go?" Juju asked.

She was standing close to me but I didn't want to step back. "I'm sure Elizabeth will be happy I'm leaving," I said.

"Don't mind her. She just had a hard time when she found out, you know?"

I didn't really know what to say about that—her girlfriend finding out about my relationship with my cousin—so we just stood in the pool of the security light for a few minutes.

"If you don't want to stay with your aunty and uncle, I understand," Juju said. "I wouldn't want to sleep there without Vivek, either. You know you can always come and stay at my house for the night."

I laughed. "Imagine what your father would say to that."

"He's traveling for work. Actually for work this time. And Mumsy knows you, and you've stayed before. It's not a problem."

"Thank you, but I'm okay. I should start going."

Juju hugged me and I hugged her back, tightly. Again, the thought came: Vivek would want me to take care of her. But I wasn't him, and I couldn't replace who he'd been to her. I didn't fit into this particular jigsaw. She waved to me after I let her go, and I waved back as I walked to the main road. I knew she was still standing there, alone under the light, watching me leave her behind.

At the bus stop, I bought a sachet of pure water and drank it slowly. It was stupid to worry about her, I told myself. She'd been coping just fine before I showed up, just like all of us. As if Vivek's parents' lives hadn't stopped, at least in every way that was important, even as they had to wake up in the morning and watch the sun move across the sky. Maybe we were all pretending to be fine because the world gave us no other option.

Suddenly I felt exhausted, completely sapped. I sat on a bench and stared out at the busyness around me. My bus came and went and I sat there, the conductor's calls of *Owere! Owere!* ringing in my skull. After its lights disappeared into the night, I reconciled myself to the fact that I'd made a decision, and I took an okada to Aunty Maja's house. It dropped me off outside the floral fence and I used the section near the gate that didn't have things growing all over it to jump the fence. I texted Juju from the back door: *I'm downstairs.* It took only a few minutes before the padlock clicked as she unlocked the iron protector and opened the door for me.

"Take off your shoes," she whispered, as she locked up again. Holding them, I tiptoed after her and we climbed the stairs, barely breathing until we were safe in her room and she'd locked the door behind us. "I'm glad you came back," she said.

I didn't reply. I was looking around the room, wondering why on earth I'd thought that Uncle Chika's house would be too painful a reminder of Vivek when the other memories were here in this house. "Maybe I shouldn't have come," I said.

"Well, it's too late." She climbed into the bed, wearing a cotton nightgown that ended above her knees. "You might as well get some sleep while you're here."

I hesitated. "What about the guest room?"

Juju sat against the pillows and wiped her face with her hand. "Osita. Please. I can't—" She opened her palms and collapsed them onto the bedspread. "I just can't."

Her eyes filled and I stepped out of my trousers, unbuttoned my shirt, and climbed into the bed in my singlet and boxers. *Take care of her. She looks so lonely.* "I'm sorry," I said, pulling her against my chest. "Shh, it's okay. I'm sorry."

She broke into sobs, muffling them against me so they wouldn't slip under the door and crawl into her parents' room. I didn't say anything. I just held her as she shook with grief, and I cried, too, but quietly, my tears wetting her hair. It was impossible not to miss him when I was with her; it was as if someone had driven a shovel into my chest, then levered it out again, taking up all it could hold, leaving a screaming mess behind. The pain thickened until I was sobbing as well, trying to shove it in the space between her neck and shoulder, my arms wrapped around her as if to save myself, not just her. I lost time inside it, plagued by the memories of the three of us there, when he was alive and happy; even of Olunne and Somto and Elizabeth there with us, when we'd all played Monopoly and Vivek cheated; when he taught us how to play solitaire with real cards; when he danced and the girls danced with him and I thought, *God forgive me, I really love him, I really do*; when he was bright and brilliant and alive, my cousin, my brother, the love of my sinful life.

It was deep into the night when I came out of it with a hiccup. We must have cried ourselves to sleep, or into some sort of stupor. Juju sniffed and sat up, her face streaked and her eyes red.

"You look terrible," I said, sitting up next to her.

"Your father," she shot back, wiping at her face.

I smiled and smoothed back some of her hair. "Are you okay?"

She leaned her head against my shoulder. "I'm fine. I haven't cried like that for him in a long time. Since I first heard."

"I hadn't cried like that for him at all."

She looked up at me. "Really?"

I nodded. There wasn't much else to say. Juju put her arm across my chest and squeezed a little, like she understood.

"What are we going to tell your mother in the morning when she sees me?" I asked.

"Don't worry, she leaves around eight. She won't disturb us." She slid off the bed and went over to her CD player.

"What are you doing?" I asked. "You're putting on music? At this time?"

Juju laughed. "Mumsy is used to it. I like to fall asleep listening to something." She slid in a Mariah Carey album, *Daydream*, skipped a song, then pressed play.

I tensed as the music started with a tinkle of chimes. "Not that one," I said. It was Juju's favorite—she used to play it all the time when Vivek was alive. It hurt to hear Mariah's voice singing over a slow piano and soft percussion, but Juju didn't turn it off. Instead, she danced slowly over, a relaxed two-step, the nightgown swirling gently around her. Her hair was down and swaying at her shoulders. "I said, not that one."

Juju climbed on the bed and straddled me. The pain in my chest was near overwhelming, but she took my face in her hands and her eyes fed on the hurt seeping out of my skin. "It's okay," she whispered. I closed my eyes because I didn't want to cry again. "It's okay." I felt her kiss me and she tasted like she was already crying. I slid my hands to her back and dug my fingers into her spine, kissing her back. I could almost feel the brush of his hair dragging over my shoulders, his strong palm on the back of my neck. Before I knew it, my tears were pooling at the corners of my mouth, she was eating them along with hers, we were filling our mouths with salt and tongues and wet grief. I pulled off my singlet and Juju raised herself enough for me to take the boxers off as well, then raised her arms to let me pull off her nightgown.

Mariah's voice was wrapping high notes around us and it felt like heartbreak washing in a thousand pinpricks over our skin. Juju leaned sideways for her bedside drawer and I kissed the arch of her neck, the wing of her collarbone, the flesh of her shoulder. She returned to my mouth and tore open the condom, lifting herself again to roll it on. I gasped when she slid back down, her knees digging into the mattress, her hands like brands burning me. I imagined Vivek behind her, his legs mixed up with mine, his mouth against her back; imagined I could reach beyond her and meet his forearms, pull him closer until we were all pressed against each other.

But when my hands reached out, there was only air, unmoving and hot.

"He's not here," Juju whispered, as if she read my mind.

I returned my hands to her, settling them on her hips as she rolled them forward.

"I know," I said. "I'm here for you."

But he was there, somehow, even if just in our memories of him—he was there because his absence was there. We didn't mind. He wouldn't have. He would have smiled that annoying little smile, lain down next to us and watched, happy. How could he be gone when he'd overtaken us so completely while he was here?

Afterward, Juju lay with her head on my chest. "I didn't tell anyone," she said quietly.

I turned my head slightly. "You didn't tell anyone what?"

"That you came looking for him the day he died. After he left here. I didn't tell your aunt."

I brought one of my hands in to stroke her shoulder. "Thank you."

"You didn't find him, abi? That's what you told me." She sounded like a little girl.

I kissed the top of her head, grateful that she couldn't see my eyes. "No," I said. "I didn't find him. Go to sleep." She snuggled in and I listened until her breathing evened out. Still, I stayed awake, staring at the ceiling, wondering if I was doing the right thing by lying. The darkness stared back at me and said nothing, as always.

Twenty

Vivek

He was right. Of course I watched them—they were so beautiful together. I put my hands on the small of her back and on the solid stretch of his chest. I kissed the sweat of her neck and his stomach.

They were keeping me alive in the sweetest way they knew how, you see.

Twenty-one

Chika repainted Ahunna's house for Vivek's burial, a bone white everywhere, drops of it splattering on the soil around the walls. Ekene had since built his own house just down the road, but Chika remained attached to their mother's house, renovating and expanding it, like a parasite customizing its host's body. In the years since her death, he had planted hedges and trees in the compound, built a fence and topped it with rolling barbed wire. He chose white even though he knew it would have to be repainted often, as dust from the untarred road coated the walls a dull, gritty red. Chika did all this in a flurry of activity, in the weeks before he collapsed into his bed and succumbed again to the familiar stupor of grief.

They all retreated to the village in those first days, Chika and Kavita and Vivek's body, Mary and Ekene; it was the only place they could be. The impending burial forced a truce between the women, for which the brothers were grateful. Osita had stayed in Owerri until the last minute, despite a heated quarrel with his parents. "I won't miss the burial," he insisted, but Ekene was so incensed by his refusal to come and help beforehand that he raised his hand to hit Osita, something he hadn't done in years. Before he could land the blow, though, he caught a glimpse of Osita's eyes, and what he saw there—complete indifference—bothered him enough to drop his arm and stalk out of the room, his rage bitter and impotent in the back of his mouth.

Once he was at the village, Ekene thought that Chika was doing too much for the burial, but he couldn't open his mouth, not when his own son was alive. He watched the repainting with grief hot in his heart, watched the bright reddening of his brother's eyes. Chika had stopped sleeping.

While Kavita lay in bed, her husband stalked through the house, among the paint buckets and brushes, the tarps spread out over the tiled floor, the rolled-up rugs and covered furniture. Everything seemed dead or suspended, everything paused, a long moment of tangible silence to mark his lost child. Vivek was resting at a local embalmer's, being prepared for his interment, as Chika walked through the night, dust layered over his skin. In the mornings Ekene brought him breakfast and made him eat it, listening as his younger brother rattled on about the burial plans. Ekene said nothing—about the repainting, the clearing of the compound, the preparations for food and music—but he drew the line when Chika mentioned killing a cow.

"Mba," Ekene said. "You can't do that." He folded his arms and stared down at his brother, who glared back up at him.

"What do you mean, I can't do that?" Chika replied. "Is it not my money? Is anyone asking you to buy the cow?"

"You're not thinking straight, and that's understandable, but let me just tell you now, Chika, you cannot kill a cow for your son. It's not right."

Chika took a deep breath. "You want to tell me what's right to bury my own son?"

Ekene sighed and sat down next to him. "He was too young, Chika. To kill a cow is to celebrate a life. That's what we do for someone who lived their whole life fully, who was not taken before his time. If you celebrate this—with a whole cow—it's like you're celebrating something unnatural, when your son died so young. Ịghọtala m?"

Chika sagged back into his chair. "I just want to honor my child," he said.

"And you can, and you will," said Ekene, putting a hand on his arm. "You know what? Kill a goat. They will even talk about that sef, but so what? Recognize your son."

"He was my only child," Chika continued. "We didn't kill a cow for Mama."

"She told us not to," said Ekene, leaning back and taking his hand off his brother. "Remember how she put it? That if she died in the evening, we should not allow the sun to rise and set on her corpse."

Chika smiled sadly. "And then she said that if we had a goat or a dog, we should slaughter it, nothing elaborate. A quiet burial. She begged us."

"And we did it the way she wanted. So how can you go and kill a cow for your son when we only killed a goat for Mama? It will look somehow."

Chika nodded. "You're right."

"Mary was saying she would just go to the slaughter-house early in the morning and buy enough meat for the people coming."

"She's organizing it?"

Ekene gave his brother a look. "Who did you think was taking care of it? Kavita?"

Chika ducked his head in shame. He'd assumed one of the women was handling those things; he hadn't even asked his wife about it. These days he found it hard to look at her, to see his grief magnified in her eyes.

Ekene softened his voice. "Mary is your sister," he said. "Kavita is in mourning, and you for some reason have decided to repaint the whole house. Of course she's taking care of it."

"I didn't even know they were talking again."

Ekene laughed shortly. "They're not, not really." He shrugged. "You know how women are."

"Please tell me that her church is not involved in this."

"Ah, no. She tried but I stopped that one. Kavita would kill her on the spot if she brought anyone from there. We're getting a Catholic priest to come to the compound."

"I'm sorry I haven't been more involved in these plans," said Chika. "Everything feels so strange around me."

"Focus on the house." Ekene was grateful that the repainting was animating his brother, even to these sleepless lengths. He still remembered what had happened after their mother died. "We will handle the rest."

The day before the burial, the repainting was complete. Ekene sent a group of young boys to the local embalmer. They returned with Vivek's body in a casket, balancing it in the back of a bus with the seats taken out, holding it steady as they trundled over bumps and potholes. When they arrived they carried it into the downstairs parlor, setting it on a table in the center of the room. Kavita watched them from the stair-case. She had been coming down before they jostled in through the door, shouting at one another to hold the casket steady. Seeing it, she sank slowly, her hands gripping the banister posts, her eyes staring through them. She heard the gentle thud as they set it down, Ekene's voice, the smack of their slippers against the tile as they filed out, some of them casting curious looks at her.

After he closed the door behind them, Ekene came and squatted on the step below her. "Kavita? Do you want to see him?"

She raised her eyes to him and he held out a hand. Heart shaking, she took it and allowed him to pull her to her feet and lead her into the parlor. The casket was still closed. Ekene let go of her hand and went to lift the lid, then stood at the head, waiting for her to walk forward. Kavita's hair was plaited into a single long braid down her back, and for a moment she imagined it was rising in the air, pulling her toward the door—because, if she didn't look inside, then maybe she could pretend that none of this was real, that Vivek was somewhere else and they'd just gotten the whole thing very wrong. But instead she walked forward and curled her fingers around the polished wood of the casket's edge. Vivek was lying inside, his hands draped along his sides, his eyes and mouth closed, his hair fanned out over a satin pillow, just as she had asked. She noticed it looked dry, his hair, and she ran her hand over it, wondering if she should pass some coconut oil through it, like she used to do.

People like to say that dead people look asleep, and maybe she would have bought that under different circumstances. Ahunna had looked asleep, but after all she had died in her sleep, so sleep and death had blurred together for her, and when they buried her the next day, she had taken peace down with her. But Kavita had already seen a different dead Vivek: the one on her veranda, the clotting blood, the flopping foot—they couldn't trick her with this cleaned-up version, they couldn't bring a peace that was never there. Not that they hadn't tried, dressing him in his favorite white traditional, his feet as bare as when he'd knocked over the flowerpot by the front door. Kavita burst into tears, her body folding in on itself, and Ekene rushed to catch her before she hit the floor. He put his arm around her and guided her weight back up to her room, murmuring nonsense that even he knew made no difference.

She came down later, this time with Chika, and they stood by the casket for a long time.

"Where's his necklace?" Chika finally said.

"I don't know. It wasn't on him when I found him."

"He was always wearing it. Are you sure it didn't fall off at the embalmer's? Or that they didn't steal it?"

Kavita's face was set, hammered hard with pain. "I'm sure, Chika. It wasn't on his body." She could tell he wanted to argue, but she knew he couldn't. She had refused to move from the body after she had found it; she had run her hands over Vivek's face and wailed with her cheek on his chest. Besides, his body had been stripped naked. If the necklace had been there, Kavita would have seen it.

"He should be buried with it. It looks somehow that he's not wearing it."

Kavita agreed and patted Chika's arm. He needed something to fixate on now that the repainting was done, now that his grief was chasing him from room to room, begging him to spend some time alone with it. They all knew what would happen when that time came: it would slice behind his knees and knock him down and he would fall back into that same dark place he'd gone when Ahunna died.

"We'll find it," Kavita said, accepting the fixation with both hands. "It has to be somewhere. He may have taken it off."

"He always wore it."

"He might have taken it off to clean it."

"Yes," said Chika. "To clean it."

They stood there, the room empty around them, before the wailers and the mourners arrived, just the two of them with their son.

Ekene had been watching them from the doorway, careful not to intrude, unwilling to break the veil of grief that had woven itself around the tableau. Eventually he left them there and went back to his house, where Mary was.

"You're not going to the wake-keeping?" he asked her.

"I'll go later," she said. "Shebi they're doing it all night?"

"The relatives, maybe. I doubt Kavita will stay the whole time. It's too painful for her."

Mary nodded. "And she won't like to be around all of them. She and Chika like to keep to themselves."

Ekene agreed, and it was close to midnight when Mary slipped out and went to join the wake-keeping. Along with the female relatives, cousins of cousins and whatnot, they covered their heads and sang gospel songs till dawn. Kavita and Chika stayed upstairs, drifting in and out of consciousness, weeping in private. One of the women brought up some food, but it stayed untouched on the tray in their room, oil congealing at the top in a lonely skin.

The Nigerwives arrived en masse in the morning, flocking around Kavita like protective birds, extending and interlocking their wings. Chika and Ekene watched them, shaking their heads.

"Maybe she will feel better with them here," said Ekene. Chika grunted in reply and his brother squeezed his shoulder.

Mary was downstairs coordinating the women who were cooking in the back. The Nigerwives' children—the ones who had come, the girls who were actually friends with Vivek—were milling about downstairs. It was only when Osita arrived that they followed him into the parlor to see Vivek's body.

Osita stood beside his cousin's casket and stared down, the wailing around him like static in the air. He felt Juju slide her hand into his, pressing her shoulder against him.

"I can't believe this," she whispered. "Should we say something?"

Osita's eyes didn't move from Vivek's face. "There's no point," he said. "He's not in there anymore."

"Osita! Don't say that!"

"It's true na. What's the point?" His voice was rough with dammed-up tears, but as angry as he sounded, he didn't step away from the casket. Juju squeezed his hand and said silent things to the body of her friend. Beside her, Olunne was praying quietly; Somto stood with them, one arm pressed across her stomach, a hand to her mouth, eyes wet.

Out back, Kavita stood on the veranda and watched as a group of men dragged a goat in on a length of frayed rope. She had asked to be called when it was time to kill the animal, and she watched as its legs were tied and a small hole dug in the ground. They laid it on its side and its bleating rang through the backyard. A knife was produced, with an old wooden handle and a sharpened although nicked blade. They pulled back the goat's head until its neck was curved, then ran the knife, almost casually, across it. Blood spouted, red and thick, pouring into the small hole in the earth. Kavita watched silently as the goat's sounds faded into gray silence. She thought of the blood on her hand when she found Vivek's body, and a wave of revulsion sent her running into the house to vomit into the nearest toilet. She heard faint laughter from the men outside and knew they were laughing at her. Maybe they didn't know she was the dead boy's mother, but it didn't matter; no one knew what it was like, what it had been like to find him.

She still had nightmares about it, though: dreams where she rushed out and there was nothing on the veranda except a widening pool of blood still enough to capture her reflection. Where he opened his eyes and laughed when she pulled back the cloth, where it was all a trick, a joke. Where she lifted his head up and he dissolved into dust in her hands, leaving her with nothing but that akwete cloth. Leaning against the porcelain of the toilet, she wondered what would have happened if someone hadn't brought Vivek back to the house, if they had just left him wherever he died. Would he have rotted there? Would anyone have cleared his body? She thought about what she owed to whoever had brought him. It killed her not to know who it was, what had happened.

Outside, she heard the crackle of the fire starting. The goat meat would be ready by the time the burial service was over that afternoon. They would make pepper soup from the entrails. Kavita flushed the toilet and closed the lid, her horror washing away in a whirlpool of blue water.

When the priest arrived, the boys who had brought the casket closed it and carried it into the compound, where a grave

had been dug next to Ahunna's. They put it down on top of two
lengths of rope, then stepped back as the priest began a short
service. The mourners sat on rented plastic chairs, or stood behind them. Kavita listened as the priest read scripture, letting
the chant of the words filter over her; she watched, numb, as he
performed the consecration of the grave. They were preparing
to take her child away, to weigh him down under so much soil.
The grave was a red yawn in the ground; the pile of dirt next to
it matched Chika's skin. If Chika stripped down and lay in the
grave, and she looked down into it, what would she see? Would
he just soak into it as if he'd been made of clay all along, molded
together with a little water, animated for her behalf so they
could have a child only to bury him?

She looked down at her hands, at the funeral program
someone had designed and printed. Probably Ekene and Mary.
She almost wished she could forgive them for the church incident. The program was full of pictures of Vivek as a small boy,
a baby; none of them looked like him now. It was as if whoever
had selected the pictures had decided to end the timeline before
Vivek had grown his hair out. Kavita didn't know whether to
be relieved that he was frozen in time this way, or annoyed that
they wanted to pretend he was someone else. She had already
heard comments, whispered things that floated up the stairs
because no one really knew how to whisper: people asking why
his hair hadn't been cut, why his parents would allow him to be
buried like that. They blamed it on Kavita, said that she was
the reason Chika was allowing things like this. She wanted to

be angry, but all she could muster was a bit of wonder that they could speak that way with his body still under the roof.

The young boys came forward again, four of them, and grabbed hold of the ropes stretched under the casket. Straining till their muscles shone, they started to lower the casket into the ground. Kavita heard Chika make a choked sound and she fumbled for his hand, tight and sweaty. The ropes jerked and slid as the casket was swallowed, the red earth blocking its dark grain. Once it hit the bottom, they dragged the ropes out from under it and took them away, coiling them up. Chika and Kavita got up to throw clods of soil into the grave, whispering their good-byes through their tears. Mary and Ekene followed them, then Osita and Vivek's friends. When everyone had done their own, the boys started to shovel the earth into the grave, filling it. Kavita walked back into the house and went upstairs. Chika stayed downstairs, fielding the visitors who pressed sympathy into his hands until his fingers felt dead.

Osita left the others in the upstairs parlor and went to walk around downstairs. He caught the sound of his mother's voice and followed it to the backyard, where they were wrapping small mounds of akpu with cling film and stacking them into coolers. Round black pots sat on squat metal frames with firewood shoved underneath, a nest of red and gray embers. The air was hot and fragrant, and the women were wiping their faces with handkerchiefs.

Mary looked up as her son made his way toward her. "Is everything all right?" she asked. She was wearing a green blouse with a gold wrapper tied over it.

Osita didn't know what to say or why he had come down. He bent and hugged her instead. It took a minute of surprise before she hugged him back. "Ehn, my son," she said. "It will be well. You hear? Don't worry. God is taking care of it." She patted his back. "It's okay. Go back inside and check on your uncle."

Osita nodded and Mary watched him leave with an overwhelming gratitude that he was alive and walking. She looked over at Vivek's grave, the soil fresh and loose, and said a quick prayer before turning back to her work.

Twenty-two

Osita didn't want to go with the girls to his aunt's house to show her the photographs. He told Juju this when she called to tell him they were going that Sunday, after church.

"Osita said he's not coming down for it," she told the other girls, gathered in Somto's bedroom.

Elizabeth shrugged. She was more than happy to not see Osita.

"Wait, repeat yourself," said Somto. "He said what?"

"That he's not coming, that we can manage it by ourselves. You know, women to women."

"Women to women wetin? Abeg, dial his number for me. What nonsense." Once she had him on the phone, Somto went straight to shouting. "Are you mad? Is this not your own aunty that we're going to see? And are you not the one who said, Oh, it's by force we must show her these pictures? My friend, you better bring yourself down here, or else I'm calling the whole thing off. Useless rat."

Osita held the phone away from his ear. "Ah-ahn, Somto, relax! You want me to come all the way just to sit there for what, thirty minutes?"

"Didn't you come just the other day when we all met up? Osita, I'm not playing with you. Vivek was your cousin. Aunty Kavita is your aunty. Don't think you can escape this one."

Olunne leaned toward the phone and chimed in, "Besides, you're in some of the pictures, so she's going to know you were involved. It's better you're there to explain yourself rather than trying to run away from it."

"We're not showing her those ones," Osita said. "Juju agreed."

"I don't actually care. If you don't come, your aunty will see those ones."

Osita sighed at her blackmailing. "Oya, fine. I'll be there."

"Sunday at three o'clock. If we don't see you, I will make everybody turn around." Somto hung up without waiting to hear Osita's reply.

Juju raised her eyebrows. "This girl, you no dey play."

"I don't have that boy's time. Let's just get this over with."

Elizabeth was snacking noisily on a pack of Burger peanuts. "Do you think we should all tell our own parents before we tell Aunty Kavita? Since we were involved."

Olunne shot her a look. "Are you mad? He was her son. How can we go and be exposing him to other people before his own mother finds out? Can you imagine how humiliated she would be?"

"Don't mind Elizabeth," said Somto. "She's just worrying

about what her parents will do if they find out about her involvement from Aunty Kavita instead of from her." Elizabeth made a face in response.

"But you know what?" said Juju. "She might not even say anything. She might want to keep it a secret."

"Or she might call everyone and shout at them," countered Elizabeth.

"We'll tell her none of our parents knew about it," said Olunne.

Her sister looked at her. "Why are you even saying it like that? They *didn't* know. It's not like we're lying."

"She might think they knew—as in, how could he get away with it under their roofs, that kind of thing."

"Come on. This is Naija. Which parents will know about something like that and not report it back to her immediately?"

The other girls nodded in agreement. What Somto said made sense. That was why they'd kept it from their parents, to protect Vivek from those who didn't understand him. They barely understood him themselves, but they loved him, and that had been enough.

Osita met them outside the gate of Chika and Kavita's house, where he was leaning against the fence with his hands digging into his pockets.

"Good," said Somto. "You're here."

He pushed himself off the fence. "Before nko? You have the pictures?"

Juju held up the envelope in response.

"Okay, let's go."

"Wait," said Olunne. "Is your uncle at home? I thought we were telling only Aunty Kavita first."

"He goes to the sports club every Sunday afternoon," said Osita. "He's started doing it again. You know he was refusing to leave the house before."

"It's good that he's there," Juju said. "My popsy said they were meeting for a drink."

Olunne nodded in relief. It was one thing to show those pictures to Aunty Kavita, even as unstable as she'd been behaving, but it was another thing completely to show them to Uncle Chika. Who knew how an Igbo man would react at seeing pictures like that of his first and only son? It was better to meet only with his mother. It was safer that way.

K avita sat them all down in the parlor without offering them anything, because they were children and they were there about Vivek and she had long since given up caring about niceties. Something in her knew that whatever they were coming to say would be a culmination of the weeks she'd spent harassing them for answers. It seeded a small anger in her. When she had told Chika they were lying, when she told their parents the children were lying, no one had believed her. Yet here they all were—even her own nephew—lined up on her sofa with their guilty faces, holding secrets behind their lips. She wanted to slap them.

The girls looked around at one another, uncertain of who should speak first. Osita was sitting apart from them in an armchair, arms folded over his stomach, looking down at the carpet. Juju felt the task should fall to her; Elizabeth and Somto would be too brash, and Olunne would be too gentle. Besides, Juju was the one holding the pictures. The envelope was hot in her hand, dragging her arm down with its weight. She rested it in her lap and turned to Kavita.

"We have something to show you," she said. "But first I want to explain why we didn't tell you about this before."

"Well, Vivek told us not to," said Somto, under her breath. They all glared at her and she raised her hands in apology, falling silent.

"We were trying to protect him," continued Juju, "and we were also trying to protect you and Uncle Chika."

Kavita was sitting with her back straight, perched on the edge of her seat cushion. Her eyes fell to the envelope Juju was holding and she put a hand on her chest as if she could calm her heart. "What's inside there?" she asked.

Juju looked at the envelope. There wasn't much point in words; the photographs would tell Kavita better than she could. She held the envelope out, her hand shaking a little. Kavita stared at it hovering in the space between them, then reached out and took it. She didn't open it at once. How could she? You can chase the truth, but who could avoid the moment of hesitation when you wonder if you really want what you've been asking for? Kavita knew that what the envelope held had power, enough to scatter her, enough for them to have held together against her for so long, even in the face of a dead child, even against her grief.

She opened the flap and pulled out the photographs. The first was a picture of Vivek in pale blue traditional, a caftan that swallowed him. His eyes were lined in black. That didn't surprise Kavita much; she'd seen him dress like that before and assumed he was mimicking the Northerners. Chika hadn't liked it and said as much, making snide remarks at the breakfast table, but Vivek had ignored them. Chika would have said more, done more, if he wasn't a little afraid of his son and his strangeness. Kavita scolded him later, after their son went out, telling him there was nothing wrong with a little eyeliner. "It starts with eyeliner," Chika had said. "Where is it going to finish? I thought you were worried about his safety, but you're just letting him walk around like that? What if someone throws a tire on him?" She dismissed his concerns and Chika stalked off, simmering impotently.

Kavita slid the top photo aside to look at the next. Juju covered her face with her hands, resting her elbows on her knees. She didn't want to watch what was going to happen. Osita looked toward the window, at the sun entering through the perforations of the lace curtains. Somto and Olunne watched Kavita, nervousness a veil over their faces, and Elizabeth picked under her nails, trying to look indifferent.

When Kavita gasped, it was like a soft blow reverberating throughout the room. She dropped the other photos in her lap and grasped the second one with both hands, staring at it. Juju had arranged them herself, so she knew which photo Kavita was holding. It was of Vivek the first time he'd worn a dress. Juju had put it near the top because he looked so happy in it; she thought that might make it a little easier for Kavita to see, that her heart might be softened because he looked so happy. She had pulled the dress from one of Maja's old suitcases, where Maja kept all the clothes she couldn't fit into anymore, along with old memories of her twenties and some photographs of old boyfriends. The dress was cinched at the waist with an A-line skirt, white and navy blue stripes running from neck to hem, short crisp sleeves, darts in the chest.

Vivek had nothing to fill out those darts, but he hadn't cared. He was spinning in the photograph, so the skirt of the dress was just a blur, like splashed water, and his hair was vague in the air. But Juju had managed to get his face in focus, and his mouth was wide open, laughing completely, his eyes squeezed shut. She had put lipstick on him, a bold red framing his teeth, and he had drawn on his eyeliner, dark on the lower lid and then a thicker line on the upper, so his eyes seemed lost in black borders.

Kavita's hands began to shake as she stared at the picture. "What is this?" she whispered, her eyes darting up to Juju's face and then to the others. The rest of them were looking down or away, anywhere but at her. Only Juju would meet her eyes, which were blurred with tears. "What is this?" Kavita repeated, her voice unsteady. "Why is he dressed like this?"

Juju was wracked with nerves, but she couldn't look away from Vivek's mother, not even long enough to draw courage from the others in the room. "He liked to dress that way," she ventured timidly. "He didn't want you to know—he didn't want you or Uncle Chika to worry about him."

"He liked to wear dresses?" Kavita dropped the photograph and picked up the rest, shock building in her face as she shuffled through them: Vivek in dresses of all kinds, sleeveless ones, short tight ones, loud printed ones, his lips painted red or pink or just glossed till they shone, his eyes always lined, sometimes with a bright splash of eyeshadow.

"My God," she said. "He was dressing like a woman?"

"He said he was dressing like himself," Somto interjected, her face resolute. "It made him happy, Aunty Kavita."

Kavita looked up slowly at them. "And all of you knew about this?" They dropped their eyes. "Even you, Osita?" Her voice was frail with betrayal when she addressed him, but Osita looked at her directly, unafraid.

"He wanted it to be kept private, so we kept it private, Aunty."

"He was sick! And you people all knew this was going on, and it didn't occur to any of you to tell me or his father? We could have helped him!"

"He didn't need help," muttered Elizabeth. Olunne kicked her in the ankle.

"Excuse me?" said Kavita.

"I said he didn't need help." Elizabeth's eyes were fixed and stubborn. "This made him happy, Aunty! He would have been worse without it. It was the only reason he was okay. So, no, we didn't tell anybody. He was our friend."

Kavita shook her head in disbelief. "No, I refuse. It must have been you girls! You dressed him up—you took advantage of him! You knew he was sick!"

Elizabeth and Somto looked like they were about to explode, but Juju stepped in gently. "It's not like that, Aunty. Vivek said it was just a part of who he was, that he had this inside him and he wanted the opportunity to express it, so that's all we gave him, that opportunity. I know it's frightening to see him look so different. I was worried, too, when he told me, when he started dressing this way. But he was so happy, it really made a difference." She smiled faintly at the memory. "I wish you could've seen him. He was happier than he'd ever been since Uncle Chika brought him back. Sometimes he asked us to call him by another name; he said we could refer to him as either she or he, that he was both. I know it sounds—"

"*Bas!*" Kavita raised her hand for silence. "It's enough. You people will not sit here and tell me my son wanted you to call him she. It's . . . it's unnatural."

"But it's true," said Elizabeth. "That's just who he was."

"That is not who my son was!" shouted Kavita, throwing the pictures to the floor. "I don't know what you people did to him, but that was not my son! That was not my Vivek!"

Osita felt his chest hurt but he didn't know what to say. He was afraid that any words leaving his mouth would emerge dripping with guilt, and he was filled with nauseous relief that Juju had agreed to take out the photos of him and Vivek. Olunne was staring at Kavita with pity. Her sister, however, was furious.

"He didn't belong to you," Somto growled, and they all looked at her, appalled. "You keep talking as if he belonged to you, just because you were his mother, but he didn't. He didn't belong to anybody but himself. And the way you're behaving now—that's why we couldn't tell you. That's why he lived the last months of his life as a secret. That's why he couldn't trust you. You think you own him, when you didn't know anything that was going on in his life."

She sucked her teeth and Kavita's tears stopped, mostly out of shock at Somto's rudeness. Olunne pinched her sister's arm to make her shut up.

"Is it me you're talking to?" Kavita said, incredulous.

"We were just trying to protect him," Elizabeth said. "We didn't want anything to happen to him. We took care of him."

Kavita turned to her. "Is that so? Where were you on the day he died, then? Where were all of you? Can someone finally answer me that one?"

A silence followed her words, heavy and thick. Then Juju spoke up reluctantly, her voice low. "He was at my house. He had started going out in dresses and I tried to stop him. I told him it wasn't safe, but he said he was just going down the road, that it wouldn't take long. Usually he'd come back quickly, but that day—" Here, Juju's voice broke. "He didn't come back at all. And there was the riot at the market—"

"And it burned down," Kavita completed, her voice flat. The akwete cloth over Vivek's body had smelled of smoke.

Juju nodded tearfully. "I think he walked too far and someone caught him," she said.

Kavita's throat clenched. She imagined the scene: Vivek caught in a mob, someone staring too much before shouting *He's a man*, bodies pressing around him, tightening like a noose, hands ripping off his clothes, someone throwing a stone that broke open the back of his head. Her boy crumpling to the ground. A sob tore through her and she folded in half to keep it in.

"Aunty Kavita! Are you all right?" Juju reached out to touch her arm.

Kavita dragged herself together, past the pain, and straightened up. "So you think that's how he died?" She directed the question to all of them. "He went out like this"—she gestured to the photographs sprawled on the floor—"and the rioters caught him?"

They all nodded. "It's the most likely scenario," Olunne said.

"Then how did he get back here?" asked Kavita. "Who brought him back?"

"Maybe it was just a Good Samaritan," said Juju. "Someone could have recognized him, and if they were too afraid to stop the attack, the least they could do was bring him home."

Kavita covered her mouth with her hand. She wanted to at least hold herself together until the children were gone. "I see," she managed to say. It wasn't as if she'd thought his death would have been anything other than violent. There was too much that was suspicious about how she'd found him: the injury, his missing clothes. Yet hearing all this, and knowing how he had been dressed when he'd gone out, knowing that he might have been lynched—it sliced her up inside.

"I should have cut his hair," she said to herself, although she didn't know what difference it would have made. Would he still have worn dresses? Eyeliner? Would life have been more dangerous if he didn't have all that hair to convince people he was a woman? She pinched the bridge of her nose with her fingers and took a deep breath.

"We're sorry, Aunty Kavita," Olunne said. "We just wanted you to know the truth."

The truth, Kavita thought. You'd think it would bring relief, after all the time she'd spent begging for answers, but instead she just felt an empty finality. It was over. Now she knew what had happened, now the mystery was solved, now they'd handed her this unknown version of her son to deal with, and it was too late to ask him any questions, to talk to him and find out what was going on, to learn about the person he'd been behind her back. It was over.

As if she could read Kavita's thoughts, Juju leaned forward. "If you have any questions about any of this, Aunty, you can always ask us. We won't keep anything from you again, we promise." She turned to glare at the others. "Right?"

They nodded quickly, their heads bobbing.

"We're telling the truth," said Elizabeth. Somto and Osita kept silent, even as they nodded their agreement. Somto was trying to stamp down her own anger; Osita was ashamed because the secret-keeping was heaviest with him. Kavita was his own aunt; if anyone should have told her, it was him. Instead he'd nailed his tongue to the bottom of his mouth and allowed

Juju to handle this whole meeting. But his shame couldn't overcome his fear; his secrets kept a padlock on his throat.

"I think all of you should get out," Kavita said, her voice tired. The children jumped to their feet, murmuring apologies. Olunne bent and picked up the photos, then put them on a side table without saying anything. She ran her fingers over them gently as she left. Kavita walked them to the door, but as she was closing it something occurred to her.

"Juju," she said. "What name was he going by? You said he sometimes wanted to be called something else."

Juju paused. "Nnemdi," she said. "The other name was Nnemdi."

Kavita nodded and locked the door behind them, the name heavy in her head. Why did it sound so familiar? She latched on to it, worried it for days, until it replaced the image of a bloodied Vivek looping in her mind.

When the name finally clicked, it startled her. She picked up the phone and dialed a number with shaking hands.

"Hello?" said a man at the other end.

"Ekene? It's Kavita."

Her brother-in-law gasped. "Kavita! Oh my God! I am so happy that you called. How are you? How is Chika?"

"Do you remember when Vivek was born?" she said, as if he hadn't said anything.

Ekene paused for a moment. "Yes, of course."

"And you said we should have given him an Igbo name, at least as a middle name?"

"I remember. Kavita, what—"

"What was that name you said we should give him?"

"Why are you—"

"Just tell me the name, Ekene. Please."

He sighed through the line. "Nnemdi. It's not a common name, but it was for Mama. Because they had that same scar on their feet." She could almost see him shrug. "If it was our father who'd had the scar, he would have been named Nnamdi, you know? But Chika didn't agree. If Vivek had been a girl, maybe he would have agreed. I don't know. He was very somehow about the whole thing, so I just left it alone. Why are you asking?"

"Did you ever tell this to Vivek?"

"No. I only talked about it once, with Chika, before the naming ceremony. That's it. What's going on, Kavita?"

Kavita felt as if the breath had been snatched out of her lungs. "Thank you," she said. "I'll call you back later." She dropped the phone on his protestations and crumpled to the floor. How had—? *If he had been a girl* . . . What did that mean now? And he had ended up a girl anyway, with the name they had denied him—ended up beaten to death and thrown in front of his own front door, and she, his own mother, had known nothing about it because he didn't trust her. Kavita sat on the floor, falling in and out of crying spells, until Chika came home and found her.

Kavita couldn't even speak. She just pointed to the photos on the side table, and watched her husband walk over to it. His body was still lean after all these years, his arms swinging easily from his shoulders, the back of his neck like a smear of clay. She watched as he picked up the stack and flipped through it, watched his eyebrows contract into a storm and his mouth open as he shouted, until his anger shook the glass in the picture frames on the wall. Then she told him what Juju and the others had told her, told him that Osita had known, and Chika raged even more, hurling the pictures away from himself until Vivek fluttered all over the parlor, settling on the carpet and sofa and side tables, his face frozen.

Kavita stared at her husband as if he was acting out her own confusion through the lines of his body. She told him their theory—that their son had died in the riot, had been beaten and stripped—and it was only then that the heat finally drained from Chika's body and he collapsed next to his wife, his face like ash. Kavita knew the images that were playing in his head, knew that his anger at Vivek's secret was washed away by the realization that someone else had killed him for it. At last, Chika dropped his head on Kavita's shoulder and wept. She put her hand to his cheek, to feel the wetness there, and murmured words she couldn't remember later.

That night, in bed, Kavita looked up at Chika from where her head was resting on his chest. "He was calling himself Nnemdi," she said.

Her husband's body stiffened.

"How did he know?" Kavita asked.

"How did he know what?" said Chika.

"That that was almost his name. Ekene said he never told him."

"When did you talk to Ekene about this?"

"Before you came home. I called him. I wanted to know how Vivek knew that name."

"You told Ekene?" Chika started to sit up, anger stirring again in him, but Kavita pushed him down.

"Don't be silly," she said. "I didn't say anything. I just asked him if he'd ever told Vivek the name and he said no. He said the name was for Mama, because of Vivek's scar. I always wondered about that."

"Ekene was being superstitious. He should know better than to repeat such nonsense to you. Forget the whole thing."

"But how did Vivek know?"

"I said forget it, Kavita!" Chika pushed her off his chest and turned over on his side, away from her.

She waited a little bit, then slipped an arm around him. "I want to visit his grave tomorrow." She felt his muscles loosen and he gave her a brief nod.

"Go to sleep, nwunye m," he said. "Enough of this name business."

The next day, they went to the village house and stood at the foot of Vivek's grave, with its large rectangular gravestone. Kavita couldn't help but imagine, for a second, Vivek's grandmother reaching out from her grave next to his, through her casket, through the soil, splintering the wood of his to take his hand. At least he was not alone. They were together, the generations before and after, gone from the here and now, leaving the rest of the family floating in life.

Kavita knelt down and ran her hand over the inscription. Something felt off, wrong. "It's our fault," she found herself saying.

Chika looked down at her. "What's our fault?"

"That he died like that, like an animal."

Her husband crouched down next to her. "Mba, it's the fault of those hooligans who did it."

"He couldn't trust us," she continued, ignoring him. "He was hiding in everyone else's house as if he didn't have a home. We didn't know anything about our own child's life."

"That wasn't Vivek. He was sick, Kavita. He was mentally unwell. That's why he was dressing like that." Chika put a hand on her shoulder but she shook it off.

"Stop saying that!"

"He was sick. He just needed more help. We should have seen it."

"You don't know what you're talking about." Kavita stood and rounded on her husband. "We don't know anything about him. You just had this your idea of who your son was *supposed* to be, and you were so busy having your affair that you missed out on his last months on earth. We can't keep insisting he was who we thought he was, when he wanted to be someone else and *he died being that person*, Chika. We failed, don't you see? We didn't see him and we failed."

Chika's face blanched as soon as she mentioned the affair.

His first instinct was to deny it, but there was no redirecting her away from the truth. He could only watch as she got to her feet, rage darkening her face, and stormed to the back door. There was a garden hoe lying there, and in a flash she grabbed it and marched back to the headstone.

"What are you doing?" he said, trying to step in front of her. But Kavita drove right past him, and then she was raising the hoe, slamming it into the headstone, the flat metal sparking against the stone.

"Kavita, *stop it!*"

She swung again and again, ignoring him, and Chika just stared, too shocked to try and restrain her. Kavita was grunting and crying—more in anger than grief, it felt like—and the gravestone chipped under her onslaught. She was aiming at the inscription now, and he cringed as he realized it.

"We—can—at—least—get—one—thing—*correct!*" she snarled between swings. Tiny cracks blossomed across the surface of the gravestone; chips littered the grass. Chika took a step back to avoid one flying into in his eye. He folded his arms and decided to let her get it out of her system. She swung until her arms were tired, then stopped, panting; the long handle of the hoe hung from her hands, banging gently against her knees. Her face was covered in sweat and her hair stuck wetly to her cheek.

"Are you finished?" he said. There was a small wound in the gravestone now, open and fragmented around the edges. Kavita whispered something and Chika took a step closer. "What is it?" She looked up at him and he wrapped his arms around her, the pain in her eyes wild and pounding. He was surprised when she didn't pull away.

"You have to fix it," she whispered, her voice thick and clotted. "You have to fix it."

Chika held her tightly. "Of course," he said, though he was confused by what exactly she meant. "I'll fix it. Of course I'll fix it."

It was only when they got home, and he made her some tea and sat with her on the veranda listening to the birds from the plumeria tree, that she finally explained what she wanted: their last gesture for their dead child, their belated apology. "He might still be alive," Kavita said, "if he'd felt safe enough to be himself in our house, instead of walking around like that. How could we protect him if we didn't know? And he told them not to tell us because he couldn't trust us, and he was right not to. Can you imagine what we would have done?"

Chika's jaw clenched, but he knew she was right. If Vivek had been alive, he would never have conceded her point, but when you've stood on ground and known your child's bones are rotting beneath you, rage and ego fade like dust in a strong wind.

"Besides," Kavita added, too calmly, "you owe me."

Eloise hung between them and Chika bowed his head, knowing he had lost. Kavita had stated her price, and his choice was clear: pay it or lose her.

He called the contractor and ordered a replacement headstone with a new inscription. He didn't tell anyone in the family about it, but he knew they visited the grave, so when Ekene called him and said, "Better late than never," Chika accepted it. He said nothing more to Kavita about his shame, or the new headstone, or the photographs. Kavita said nothing to him when she took them out of the drawer and arranged them in an album, which she hid under her side of the mattress. She pored over it for hours when Chika was out of the house, trying to find the child she'd lost, trying to commit to memory the child she'd found.

Twenty-three

Osita

I went to Vivek's grave on his birthday, very early in the morning.

I knew Uncle Chika and Aunty Kavita were going to arrive later that day and spend the night, so I came the day before and slept in my grandmother's room. When it was dawn, just the earliest part of it, the cracks in an eggshell before it splinters open, I went out into the compound and stood in front of his grave, with the new marker Aunty Kavita had forced Uncle Chika to put in. He hadn't had much of a choice after she tried to destroy the old one.

The air around me was damp, dew clinging to the grass and the leaves, and at the head of the grave the small star fruit tree, struggling out of being a seedling. I wasn't sure why Aunty Kavita had picked a fruit tree that would feed on Vivek's body. Uncle Chika probably would have selected something else, like a palm tree. Did she look forward to the day when it would actually have star fruits hanging from its branches? Would she pick them and eat them as if she was absorbing him, bringing him back inside where he'd come from? It would be something like Holy Communion, I imagined, body and blood turned into yellow flesh and pale green skin, bursting with juice. Or maybe she would never touch the fruit—maybe no one would—and they would fall back to the ground to rot, to sink back into the soil, until the roots of the tree took them back and it would just continue like that, around and around. Or birds would show up and eat the fruit, then carry Vivek around, giving life to things even after he'd run out of it himself.

I squatted next to the grave, my legs still tired from sleep, then gave up and sat down on the marker after looking around to make sure no one was there. I had brought a black-and-yellow polythene bag with me, knotted firmly. Sitting on my cousin's grave, I started to work the knot loose. It was tight; I had wrenched it closed with shaking hands, planning to burn it, certainly never to open it again. Then it had stayed under my bed in my room for months. Sometimes I would bring it out and hold it to my chest, fighting the urge to rip it open. I always put it back. But today; today's own was different.

It took me a few minutes and the application of my teeth for me to get it open, and then I parted the plastic mouth and folded the bag back. Lying inside was a dress, made of soft cotton, except for the parts that had stiffened with old blood. I had folded it carefully when I put it into the bag, and now I smoothed the square it made in my lap. It was a deep blue, like what I imagined falling into the sea would look like if you kept trying to find the bottom. There were red hibiscus flowers splashed all over it, yellow dots quivering at the stamens. They hadn't been printed to scale; these hibiscus were smaller than real ones would be, so that more of them could fit into the blue. It had been Vivek's favorite dress.

He was wearing it in one of the pictures Juju was going to show Aunty Kavita, but I had taken it from her room the morning after we all met at the sports club, so that one never made it to Aunty Kavita. Juju was still asleep when I left and I didn't wake her up. Saying good-bye would have been too much, too somehow, given what had happened that night. So I had walked quietly across the bedroom floor to pick up my boxers and trousers, balancing carefully as I put them on, then wearing my crumpled shirt and singlet. Juju's bag was lying on her dressing table and I reached inside it with a delicate hand, fishing out the photo envelope. I flicked through the pictures quickly, looking for the one I'd seen at the sports club. The girls had seen that particular picture, too, but they knew Vivek and they would have thought he was just playing around, as he often did with us. Maybe it was my guilt making me paranoid, but that photograph felt like exposure, and I couldn't let my aunt see it. God forbid. If she told my parents about it, I couldn't begin to imagine the consequences.

In the picture, Vivek was wearing the dress, a wraparound tied on the left of his waist. The neckline fell into a V, showing the bone of his sternum. His hair was down and falling around his face. Juju had combed and plaited it with gel into a hundred small plaits, then let them dry and released them into many small waves cascading down his body. He was sitting in my lap with his legs crossed, the dress riding high on his thighs, his torso leaning forward as he laughed into the camera. One arm was around my neck and I was looking at his face. My expression made me cringe. It was, for lack of a better word, adoring. Unfettered. As if there was no danger of anyone seeing me gaze at him like that. As if we were alone and I wasn't afraid and we weren't cousins and any of this wasn't terrifying.

Vivek had shaved his chest and legs—he did that often in those last few months—and his toes were painted a red that matched the flowers on his dress. I remembered the first time I saw him in that dress; I was surprised at its long sleeves and shoulder pads. It would have been almost demure if not for the neckline, which he would cover with his hair. But he spun around to show it off, and for once he looked happy and not tired, not like he was dying or suffering. I couldn't help but be happy for him. I had surrendered by then, you see, and we were in Juju's house, in our bubble where everything was okay and the outside world didn't exist. Sitting on his grave with the dress in my hands, I felt the weeping churn in my chest.

Everything would have stayed okay if he hadn't left the bubble. If he hadn't felt the need to start going outside and putting himself at risk. How were we supposed to protect him if he wouldn't stay inside?

On the day the market burned, I had gone to Juju's house to look for him. She told me he'd gone out again. I had shouted at her, unfairly, as if I didn't know she couldn't stop him. No one could stop him—we had all tried already, many times. I went out, jumped on an okada, and set out to look for him. I knew he liked to visit one woman near the market who sold puff-puff, so I told the okada man to go down Chief Michael Road. We had just passed the first junction when we heard the noise and saw the crowd in the distance. My okada swerved to the side of the road and stopped.

"Commot, commot!" shouted the driver.

"You're not going again?" I asked.

"You dey craze? You no dey see riot? My friend, commot, make I go. Keep your money sef."

Grumbling and cursing, I got off and he sped away. I sighed and looked around and that was when I saw Vivek a few blocks down, unmistakable in that dress. I called his name but he didn't turn around and so I ran to him, pushing his shoulder when I reached him.

"You don't hear your name?!"

My cousin turned and looked at me calmly. "I'm Nnemdi," she corrected.

I wiped my face with my hand. Today of all days. "Okay, sorry, Nnemdi. Please, can we go back to Juju's house?"

"No problem. But I want to get some puff-puff first."

I stared at her, then gestured to the mayhem ahead of us. "You want to enter that? For puff-puff?"

She looked at the crowd and her face wavered. She was twisting her hands together like she did when she was nervous. "It won't take long. Can we go after I buy it?" she said.

I wanted to shout at her, but the last time I did that in

public, she had threatened to punch me in the face, then ran away. I wasn't able to chase her—it would've looked too somehow—so I went back to Juju's house and waited till she came back on her own. This time, I gently held her shoulders and looked into her eyes. The cotton of the dress was soft under my palms. "Nnemdi," I said. "I'm sure even the woman selling it has packed her things and gone already. She won't be there. Everyone is going, see."

A plume of smoke was rising against the horizon from the market. The road beside us was packed with speeding vehicles, buses and taxis and private cars. A trader carrying folded yards of cloth piled precariously around her zoomed past on an okada. It was weaving through the other vehicles, and as it passed us, it swerved to avoid a pothole and some of the cloth fell off, landing in a cloud of sand. The woman shouted at the okada driver to stop, but he didn't, shouting back at her as he continued to speed away from the brewing mob.

"We have to go," I told my cousin. "Biko, before something happens to you."

She glared at me. "Why is it me you think something will happen to? You nko?"

"Please, don't start this now. You know it's not even safe for you to be going out of Juju's house like this, let alone in this area, let alone in this situation! Don't act stupid. Let's go!"

"I see." Her face had settled into coldness. "So now you think I'm stupid?"

"Nnemdi, please. You can fight me when we reach Juju's house. Let's just go. Biko."

"You're ashamed of me," she said, her voice surprised. "That's why you don't like me going out like this. It's like you're always ashamed, Osita. First of yourself, then of us, now of me."

"Jesus Christ. That's not true. Abeg—"

"No, it's true. You don't mind anything when we're inside and nobody can see us, but that's why you don't like me to go outside like this. You don't want anyone to see me. Or is it that you don't want them to see me with you?"

I groaned and clutched at my head. We didn't have time for this. What would happen if someone looked too closely at her, someone holding a machete and buffeted by a mob? How quickly they could hurt her, kill her. I grabbed her arm and started to drag her away. "We don't have time to be quarreling on the road!"

She tried to pull away and started hitting me. "Let me go! Hapu m aka!!"

I lost it. "*We have to go now!* Do you know what they'll do to you?"

Nnemdi gasped and wrenched away from me with all her strength, breaking my hold. I was startled by the pain in her eyes, surprised that the truth could hurt her so much. She pulled herself away with such force that she stumbled, and her heel caught on a stone, and she fell. It happened so fast. I saw her head strike the raised cement edge of the gutter at the side of the road. I saw her body slump, eyes closed, blood pooling into the sand within seconds.

I screamed.

"No no no *no!*" I ran and knelt by her, sliding one hand

under her neck to lift her head up. "Nnemdi. Nnemdi!" Maybe she wouldn't recognize that name after hitting her head. "Vivek," I whispered. "Vivek, open your eyes. Please, bhai. Open your eyes." My hand was now wet with blood—there was so much blood. Panic was a vulture inside my body, trying to get out, pecking and flapping wildly at me. I looked around and scrabbled to get the cloth that had fallen from the okada. I ripped off the plastic covering and lifted her neck again, using the cloth to try and stop the bleeding.

Hospital. I needed to get her to a hospital. No one around me was paying attention; everything was chaos; people were running all around us. I lifted Nnemdi and carried her against my chest, using my upper arm to cushion her head. I stood at the side of the road and an okada skidded in front of me. The driver was, unexpectedly, a woman.

"Wetin happen?" she asked, staring at Nnemdi.

"She fell down. Please, can you take us to a hospital?"

She nodded. "Enter," she said, and I climbed up behind her, carefully, sitting far back enough so Nnemdi could fit. We sped off.

"Anyangwe Hospital," I called out to the driver. "Do you know it?" It was just around the corner from Uncle Chika's house, walking distance. I could run and get them while the doctors took care of Nnemdi. The driver nodded and I bent my face to Nnemdi's, wind whistling past us. "Wake up," I begged. "Wake up for me." We wove through cars and I kept my arms clutched tightly, her knees draped over the crook of my elbow. Her shoes fell off and I didn't care. When we reached the junction of a side road leading to the hospital, a giant pothole filled with water blocked most of the road. The okada stopped at the edge.

"My bike no fit enter that one," she said. "E go spoil my engine. We can go around by the main road. Abi the hospital is just there?"

"No wahala," I said, carefully climbing down. "I can walk from here. Ego ole?"

She waved her hand. "Forget the money. Go and make sure your wife is all right."

I nodded, tears solid in my eyes, and she drove away as I waded through the edge of the puddle. The side road was a shortcut, small and narrow, unpaved, shadowed by trees. I knew this small road well—there was a side gate from Uncle Chika's compound that opened up into it. When Vivek and I were still in secondary school, we had broken the rusty padlock and cleared a path so that we could use the gate to sneak out of the compound. I got through the puddle, legs wet to my calves, and I was passing the gate when I looked down at Nnemdi and stopped.

There was something new in her face. It didn't look like her anymore. Hurrying, I knelt down and laid her on the ground to check her neck for a pulse. There was nothing. I held my hand in front of her nose. Nothing. My sleeve and shirt were soaked in blood. I couldn't breathe. My eyes blurred and I felt as if I was going to faint. I shook her, called both her names, as if it would do anything. We were under a flame-of-the-forest tree. An orange flower fell down and landed on her chest.

I knelt there, close to the fence, no one else on the road with me. I put my hand on her face and called her names again. It felt as if I was imagining the whole thing.

I was there on the road with my cousin's body in front of me. Someone was going to see me.

The thought took precedence and adrenaline shot through me. I can't tell you why I did what I did next, except that Uncle Chika's house was right there, and I knew the hospital was now useless, and I didn't know how I would answer any of their questions if I walked into either place. Vivek had always told me and Juju, "Make sure my parents don't find out. They already have so much to deal with. Make sure they don't find out about Nnemdi."

So I did what he would have wanted me to do.

I untied the bow the dress was fastened with, and I stripped it off her body, crying the whole time, my hands shaking, my head scattered. I took the material I had used to soak up the blood and unfolded it. It was akwete, in a red-and-black pattern. I used it to cover my cousin and I picked her up again, and I walked to the side gate—the lock was never fixed—and pushed it open with my foot. I ran through the backyard, along the side of the house to the veranda, where I laid Nnemdi down by the welcome mat. There was so much blood, all over both of us. I couldn't stop crying.

"I'm sorry," I whispered. "I'm so sorry." I stroked some hair off her face and pressed my forehead against hers, my tears falling on her nose and mouth. My uncle's voice sifted through the window.

"Did you hear that?" he was asking my aunt.

"Someone is at the door?" she replied.

I choked back a sob, sniffed, and held my cousin's face in my hands, kissing her lips. "I have to go," I told her. "Please, forgive me. I have to go."

I reached around her neck and unfastened her silver chain, the Ganesh pendant still warm against my palm. I clenched my fingers into a fist around it.

"I love you," I said to her silent eyes. Then I got up and ran, bent in half so I couldn't be seen through the windows. I ran away, through the back, through the side gate, pausing only to close it behind me. I ran down the side road and picked up the dress from the ground, shaking off the orange and yellow petals that had accumulated on it. I ran down to the main road, past the hospital gates, and people stared at me, but the grief on my face must have looked familiar this close to the hospital, as if I had lost somebody there. I asked a woman selling oranges at the side of the road for a polythene bag. She stared at the blood on my clothes in alarm, but she gave me a black-and-yellow bag and handed me a sachet of pure water.

"Clean your face," she said. "Gịnị mere gị?"

"I was in an accident," I said, as I rinsed myself, pale red water in my hands.

"Chineke! Are you okay?"

"Yes, Ma. I'm just trying to reach home."

"There's plenty blood on your shirt."

"It's not my own."

"It's not good to be walking around looking like that." She

called out to a woman selling clothes in a kiosk next to her, gaudy bedazzled T-shirts and ankara dresses hanging off bone-white headless mannequins. "Vero! Biko, nyem shirt for this boy."

The woman stuck her head out of her kiosk. "Fifty naira!" she called back. I dug into my pocket and pulled out a hundred, handing it to the orange-seller. She looked at me in surprise, then waved it at the other woman, who nodded and came out with a black T-shirt that had a bedazzled crown on it. "This one will enter him," she said. The orange-seller gave her the hundred naira and received fifty back. She tried to give it to me but I shook my head. "It's okay, Ma." I put the bag between my knees and took off my shirt right there on the road, pulling on the black one. It was a little tight but it fit. I put my bloody shirt and Nnemdi's dress into the bag, and when I looked up, both women were staring at me.

"That's how you just naked yourself outside your house?" said the clothes-seller.

"Mind your business," the orange-seller told her. "Get home safe, you hear?" she said to me, and I nodded.

"Daalụ, Ma."

There was still blood drying on my jeans, but they were dark, so they didn't show much. I went straight to the bus stop and took a bus to Owerri. When I paid the conductor, some of the notes were stained with blood, but he didn't even blink.

My parents weren't home when I reached the house, so I took the key from under the mat and let myself in. I had enough time to take a bath and burn my bloodied clothes with the rubbish in the backyard, which I was supposed to burn anyway. I don't know why I kept the dress, knotting it into that bag and putting it under my bed. I rinsed the necklace and kept it under my mattress, even though I risked my mother finding it if she came into my room. It was unlikely that she would. I couldn't bury it—I just couldn't.

I still remember the blood washing down the drain of the bathtub as I poured containers of water over my body, scrubbing myself until the water was clear and then pouring and scrubbing even more, going through buckets and buckets, until I had used all the water in the bathroom drum. I dried myself with a white towel, to make sure that not a drop of my cousin was left on me, then fetched water to refill the drum. Then I left the house, knowing it was only a matter of time before Uncle Chika would call to tell my father what had happened, and I didn't want to be there to pick the call.

When I came home late that night, my parents were weeping in the sitting room. When they told me, I wept with them as if it was my first time.

I have pretended every day since then. I pretended with the girls and at the burial and with everyone. It was why I didn't go to see anyone, why I stayed in Owerri. I needed to learn how to behave with this secret dropping petals inside me like this. I helped Aunty Kavita look for the necklace after she got me from Port Harcourt, as if I wouldn't go home and pull it out, press it against my mouth, and choke back my sobs so that my parents wouldn't hear.

When we told Aunty Kavita our theory that Vivek had

gone out as Nnemdi and someone must have killed him during the riot, I could barely talk, my throat was swelling up so much. They thought it was grief. "The boys were very close," my aunt said afterward, finally allowing other people the right to mourn her child. I listened to them wonder what had happened to the dress, knowing the whole time that it was hidden under my bed, soft and stiff. I watched my aunt cry as she imagined the suffering her Vivek had endured. I wanted to tell her that Nnemdi didn't feel anything from the moment she fell, that she was asleep in my arms when she died, that there wasn't pain like that, but I couldn't say anything. I didn't say anything. We had told her as much truth as she could handle. I was keeping the rest for myself.

So there I was with the dress, at the grave, sitting there as the sun washed up in diluted yellow. I didn't know what time my aunt and uncle would arrive. I felt like I was always running just a few steps ahead of them, holding secrets they couldn't catch up to. I picked up a hoe that was lying by the back door and dug carefully at the base of the little star fruit tree, deep enough so that rain wouldn't wash it open, trying to hack the roots apart. I used my hands to dig the rest, around the roots, making small excavations, pouring water into it to soften the soil. When it was deep enough, I took the dress out of the bag. I held it to my face, trying to smell my cousin's skin, trying not to smell the dried blood. It smelled like nothing much. I put it inside the hole and buried it, then shifted sand and leaves on top so they wouldn't see that something had been buried there.

"I'm so sorry," I told the grave. "It was an accident. I would never have hurt you, not in a thousand years. I swear to God. You were my brother and I loved you. I only wanted to protect you."

I put my hand on the cement and it was cold. "I miss you every single day."

My voice broke and the grave said nothing back. I knelt there for a long time, and finally I stood up and dusted the dirt off my knees. The sun was stronger in the sky now. I wiped my eyes and picked up the polythene bag. Holding it tight in my hand, I pulled the photograph of us out of my back pocket. I had considered burying it as well, but I couldn't; I couldn't let everything rot in that grave with my cousin. I stroked my thumb across the glossed surface before putting it back in my pocket with the necklace. Then I walked away, knowing that I would be leaving, going far away, to somewhere I could put his charm around my neck and wear it every day, and maybe then it would feel like he hadn't left me after all.

Twenty-four

Nnemdi

I often wonder if I died in the best possible way—in the arms of the one who loved me the most, wearing a skin that was true. I watch him grieve and I want to tell him he's already been forgiven for everything and anything he could ever do to me. I want to tell him that I knew I was dancing with death every day, especially when I walked outside like that. I knew it, and I made my choices anyway. It wasn't right or fair, what happened, but it wasn't his fault. I want to thank him for loving me.

My mother has changed the inscription on my grave. She could smell that it was a lie. Love and guilt sometimes taste the same, you know. Now it says:

VIVEK NNEMDI OJI
BELOVED CHILD

I wonder if anyone is pleased that I finally got my Igbo name. If my grandmother, floating somewhere here with me, is happy to be acknowledged at last. I would say it was too late, but time has stopped meaning what it used to.

I don't mind anymore. I see how things work now, from this side. I was born and I died. I will come back.

Somewhere, you see, in the river of time, I am already alive.

Acknowledgments

To the authors whose books helped me write this one—Toni Morrison for *Love* and Gabriel García Márquez for *Chronicle of a Death Foretold*—thank you. To the Nigerwives, for the childhood you made possible, full of books and waffles and swimming and friends. Thank you all for being there, especially Aunty Ingrid and Aunty Helga, and a particular shoutout to Aunty Vonah, for helping me become a writer. To the original crew—JK and Franca, Julie and Chiji and Chukwuma—thank you for the brilliant times, the games, and all the magic. To the entire city of Aba, my home for sixteen years. To Ekenna Avenue and Okigwe Road. To the Aba Sports Club—greet the suya guys for me. What a world it was. To all the queer and gendervariant people back home, especially those making new worlds for us, jisie ike. What a world it will be.

To my brilliant editor, Cal Morgan, and my legend of an agent, Jackie Ko, as well as all the other wonders at the Wylie Agency—Sarah, Emma, Alba, Ekin, and Jessica. To Jynne and everyone else at Riverhead Books. Thank you all for being such a stellar team. To Eloghosa Osunde and Ann Daramola for reading and loving this book so early—thank you, godsiblings. To my dear Christi Cartwright, I am so grateful for the time and care you put into this.

It has taken several people to bring *The Death of Vivek Oji* into readers' hands, and my appreciation goes out to each and every one of you. We need all of us to bring these stories into the world. I'm glad to be doing this work with you.